"I knew I could

"I'm so exhausted a[...]
sad," Maya said. "Th[...]

"I haven't really don[...]
tightened his arms [...]

"You were there," she said. "When I kissed you earlier, I wasn't really planning on that. It caught me off guard." Her eyes met his and he felt a fresh jolt of heat. "But I'm not sorry it happened."

"No," he said. "I'm not sorry, either."

"Everything about the past two days is a little unreal," she said. "Including you."

She was offering him an easy out—a safe way to dismiss what had passed between them and make it about the heat of the moment. But for once he didn't want that.

He kissed her—just a brief brush of his lips across hers, then he stepped back. "Oh, I'm real all right."

AVALANCHE OF TROUBLE

CINDI MYERS

HARLEQUIN INTRIGUE®

For my nieces, Morgan and Kelli

ISBN-13: 978-1-335-52654-0

Avalanche of Trouble

Copyright © 2018 by Cynthia Myers

Recycling programs for this product may not exist in your area.

Printed in U.S.A.

Cindi Myers is the author of more than fifty novels. When she's not crafting new romance plots, she enjoys skiing, gardening, cooking, crafting and daydreaming. A lover of small-town life, she lives with her husband and two spoiled dogs in the Colorado mountains.

Books by Cindi Myers

Harlequin Intrigue

Eagle Mountain Murder Mystery

Saved by the Sheriff
Avalanche of Trouble

The Ranger Brigade: Family Secrets

Murder in Black Canyon
Undercover Husband
Manhunt on Mystic Mesa
Soldier's Promise
Missing in Blue Mesa
Stranded with the Suspect

The Men of Search Team Seven

Colorado Crime Scene
Lawman on the Hunt
Christmas Kidnapping
PhD Protector

The Ranger Brigade

The Guardian
Lawman Protection
Colorado Bodyguard
Black Canyon Conspiracy

Rocky Mountain Revenge
Rocky Mountain Rescue

Visit the Author Profile page at Harlequin.com.

CAST OF CHARACTERS

Maya Renfro—A high school teacher from Denver, Maya finds herself thrust into a small-town mystery when her sister and brother-in-law are murdered and she has to protect her niece. All she wants is to get back to her exciting life in the big city, but a murderer—and a charming sheriff's deputy—may change her plans.

Deputy Gage Walker—Sheriff Travis Walker's younger brother has a reputation as a carefree ladies' man devoted to his job, but Maya and her niece have him looking at life differently. When they're in danger, he's forced to make difficult choices.

Angela and Greg Hood—Maya's sister and her husband had plans to develop their newly purchased mining claim as a demonstration project before they were brutally murdered.

Casey Hood—As the only witness to her parents' murder, Casey is hunted by a killer, but she proves more resourceful than anyone could have expected.

Henry Hake—The real-estate developer went missing a month ago. So who is behind the mysterious goings-on at the once-dormant development site?

Wade Tomlinson—The climbing guide and part owner of an outdoor store helps with the search for Casey and may have information about her parents' murderer.

Brock Ryan—Wade's business partner is dating a mystery woman and has been spending a lot of time out of town lately.

Ed Roberts—The old hermit is a convicted sex offender and general grouch—is he also a murderer?

Chapter One

Gage Walker wouldn't have said he was a superstitious man, but he didn't believe in tempting fate. Don't brag about your bank account being full or a big bill will surely show up in the mail that will tap you out. Don't plan a fishing trip in April and leave the rain gear at home just because it was sunny when you left the house. Don't complain about being bored at work or you'll get a call that will have you working overtime for the next week.

When your work was as a sheriff's deputy in a small, rural county, boring was good, or so he always reminded the rookies and reserve cops. Boring meant crime was down and people were happy. The adrenaline rush of a real crime might make your day go faster, but it also meant someone was hurt, or had lost something valuable to them, or, worst of all, someone was dead.

The man and the woman in this camp up near Dakota Ridge were definitely dead, each shot in the back of the head, execution-style. They were both in their early thirties and had probably been a nice-looking

couple before someone had tied their hands behind
their backs and sent a bullet through each of their
brains. The driver's license in the man's wallet identi-
fied him as Greg Hood, from Denver.

Judging by the matching gold wedding bands they
wore, Gage guessed the woman was Greg's wife. The
couple hadn't been killed for money. The man's wallet
still had cash and credit cards in it, and in addition to
the wedding rings, they both wore expensive-looking
watches. They had been left lying on the forested floor
between their tent and the cold remains of a campfire, eight miles from the nearest paved road, about
a hundred yards from the late-model SUV registered
in their name.

"Creepy." Gage's fellow deputy, Dwight Prentice,
came to stand next to Gage, staring down at the bodies. Dwight looked around them, at the still forest,
lodgepole pine and aspen so thick in places a man
could scarcely walk between the trunks, the evergreen-
scented air now tainted with the stench of death.

"Yeah, it's creepy," Gage said. "If someone had it
in for these two, why not kill them in Denver?" To his
way of thinking, murder belonged in the city, not in
the peaceful mountains where he had been born and
raised and made his home.

Though he had been a member of the Rayford
County Sheriff's Department for four years now, Gage
hadn't seen death like this before. People in Eagle
Mountain—the county's only town—died peacefully
of old age, of diseases or a heart attack, or maybe
after a fall while climbing or hiking in the surround-

ing mountains. A little over three years ago, a young lawyer in town had been murdered. People still talked about that case; it had been so unusual for the quiet community that primarily made its living from tourists.

This case was going to give everyone something more to talk about. "I'll drive down in a few minutes and call this in," Gage said. No company had thought it worthwhile to build cell towers on Dakota Ridge, so this corner of the sheriff's department jurisdiction had no coverage, and the radio wasn't much more reliable. Besides, talking about something like this over the radio pretty much guaranteed that half the town would know about it, since so many of them made a hobby out of listening to police scanners. They would be out here to sightsee before the crime scene techs had even finished pulling on their Tyvek suits.

"I want to have another quick look around first." This was his last chance to size up the scene for himself, before the techs and photographers, ambulance personnel and reporters trampled everything into dust. Oh, they'd do all the right things—cordon off the scene and establish an entry corridor—but never again would the scene look like this, unmarred by tape and markers and footsteps.

Moving carefully, Gage stepped around the tent and bent down to look inside. "Who called this in, do you know?" Dwight asked. He remained standing near the bodies.

"Milo Werth called it in," Gage said. "Said he saw the car parked here two days ago when he delivered propane to Windy Peak Ranch, at the end of the road. He came by this morning to pick up a heeler pup Jim Trotter at Windy Peak had for sale and said the car looked like it hadn't moved. With the pup and his little boy in the truck, he didn't want to stop and look, but thought we should check it out." He unhooked the collapsible baton from his utility belt and extended it, then used it to pull back the tent flap.

Inside was a jumble of sleeping bags, a plastic tote with a lid, and a scattering of clothes. A battery-operated lantern hung from a hook at the center of the tent's dome, and a backpack sat propped to the left of the door. Then he spotted a woman's purse next to the backpack. He pulled out a camera and took a picture of it in place, then pulled on latex gloves and, using the baton, hooked the straps of the purse and carefully lifted it out.

"Looking for ID?" Dwight asked.

"I'm looking for anything that tells me why they were up here."

"That's easy enough to figure out," Dwight said. "They came up here to camp. A nice break from city life."

"Except this isn't National Forest or BLM land," Gage said as he pulled a red leather wallet from the purse. "This is private property. This whole area is patented mining claims."

"Maybe they didn't know that," Dwight said. "Maybe they thought they could pull over anywhere and camp. Nobody bothered them, so they thought it was all right."

"Maybe." The sheriff's department had been called in before to explain to clueless campers that even if the land they were on wasn't occupied, it wasn't free for them to set up camp. Gage opened the wallet and studied the driver's license in the little plastic window opposite the checkbook. Angela Hood had been a pretty brunette with long, straight hair, green eyes and a wide smile. She was thirty-two years old, five feet five inches tall. Gage flipped through the credit cards and store loyalty cards in their clear plastic sleeves next to the license and stopped when he came to a bright yellow card. *In Case of Emergency, Contact Maya Renfro, (sister).* A phone number and address were neatly printed in the space below.

Gage made note of the number, then dropped the wallet back into the purse and replaced the purse inside the tent. "I got a number for her emergency contact," he said. "Looks like it's her sister."

"You could let Travis contact her." Travis Walker was the Rayford County sheriff—and Gage's older brother.

"No, I'll do it," Gage said. Not that he looked forward to telling a woman her sister had been murdered, but he hoped Maya Renfro could lend some insight into what Angela and Greg had been up to that might have gotten them killed.

He made his way back around the tent to the rough track that led into the clearing. "I'll be back as soon as I make the call," he told Dwight.

"I'll be here."

Gage took another look at the SUV parked at the road—a dirty white, late-model Chevy with a cooler and a black plastic garbage bag in the rear compartment. The couple had probably stashed the food and garbage there as a precaution against bears, which showed they were savvy campers. The techs would go over the vehicle, but to Gage, it looked as if it hadn't been touched. And he spotted no other shoe or tire impressions in the soft soil on the verge of the road. So how had the killers gotten to the site?

He went over the details of the crime scene in his head as he drove the eight miles back to the highway. Once he had a strong phone signal, he parked on the shoulder and called the sheriff's department. "Gage, I've been calling you for the last half hour. Where have you been?" Adelaide Kinkaid, the police department's office manager, or, as she liked to refer to herself, "the woman who keeps everything going around here," addressed Gage as if he was a sixteen-year-old delinquent instead of a twenty-five-year-old cop. But Adelaide talked to everyone that way. It was part of her dubious charm.

Gage ignored her question. "Is Travis in?"

"No, he is not. When I couldn't get hold of you, he had to go over to the high school to take a theft report."

"Fine. I'll call his cell."

"But where—"

Gage ended the call. Later, he would no doubt get a lecture from Adelaide about it being his responsibility to keep her informed of his whereabouts, but annoying her now was worth a little aggravation later.

Travis answered Gage's call on the second ring. "What's up?" the sheriff asked. Two years older than Gage, he had won a hotly contested election two years previously to become the youngest county sheriff in Colorado. Since then, even the detractors who had tried to hold his youth against him had admitted to being impressed with his performance. Gage hadn't been surprised at all—Travis had always been the more serious and determined of the three Walker siblings. Gage, though equally smart and athletic, preferred a more laid-back approach to life.

But there was nothing laid-back about his current situation. "We've got a mess on our hands," he said. "That abandoned car Milo Werth called in belongs to a young couple who got themselves killed up on Dakota Ridge."

"Killed?" A sound like Travis closing a door. "How?"

"Shot in the back of the head. Execution-style— hands tied behind their backs. Greg and Angela Hood, from Denver. They were camping on land up there— probably a mining claim."

"Who owns the claim?" Travis asked.

"I haven't got that far yet. We need to call in the crime scene techs. And depending on what they find, we may need to get some help from the state. Everything about this feels bad to me."

"I'll call CSI as soon as we get off the phone," Travis said. "You head back up there and guard the crime scene."

"Dwight's up there now. I found a next of kin notification card in the woman's wallet. I figure I'll make that call before I head back up. Says it's her sister."

"Hard," Travis said.

"Yeah, but it needs to be done. And if it was our sister, I'd want to know right away."

"Agreed," Travis said. "Fortunately, I talked to Emily this morning. She was on her way to class." Their baby sister was working on her MBA in economics at Colorado State University.

"Good to know. Tell the forensics team there's a pull-off just after mile marker eight. I want it checked for any tire impressions or other evidence. There aren't any signs near the Hoods' car, so I'm wondering if the killers parked there and walked up."

"Will do."

The call ended, Gage pulled up the number for Angela Hood's sister. A woman answered the phone. "Hello?" Her voice was raised to be heard over what sounded like a crowd.

"This is Deputy Gage Walker with the Rayford County Sheriff's Department," Gage said. "Is this Maya Renfro?"

"Speaking." A cheer rose up behind her, momentarily drowning her out.

"I can hardly hear you," Gage said. "Where are you?"

"High school gym. Hang on a minute." The crowd noise rose again, then was abruptly cut off. "I ducked into the locker room," Maya said. "This should be better."

"You're in high school?" Cold sweat beaded on the back of Gage's neck. It was hard enough giving bad news to an adult, but to hurt a teenager that way? "Maybe you should get a teacher in there with you. I can wait."

"*I'm* a teacher," Maya said. "Who did you say you were again? I didn't catch it."

"Deputy Gage Walker with the Rayford County Sheriff's Department."

Silence. He tried to picture her—probably dark-haired, like her sister, with the same green eyes and open face. "Ms. Renfro?" he prompted.

"What's happened?" she asked, her voice strained. "Why are you calling me?"

"You have a sister—Angela Hood?"

"Has something happened to Angie? What's happened to her?"

Better to get this over with. There was no way to cushion the blow. "I'm sorry to tell you your sister is dead."

More silence. No screaming or crying. Gage waited. He could hear her breathing, hard, on the other end of the line. "What happened?" she asked finally, her voice hoarse with unshed tears.

"She and her husband, Greg Hood, were shot and killed at their campsite near here."

"Shot? I don't understand? Was it hunters? Some kind of accident?"

"It wasn't an accident. Did your sister and her husband have any enemies? Anyone who would have wanted to kill them?"

"No! Are you saying they were murdered? While camping?"

"That's what it looks like. Do you know why they were here?"

"They bought the land a few weeks ago and wanted to spend some time on it. They said it was really beautiful up there. Who killed them?"

"We don't know yet. Did either of them mention having an argument or disagreement with anyone? Did they mention arranging to meet someone up here?"

"No. It was just a quick trip to get the lay of the land and make plans."

"What kind of plans?"

"Casey!" She choked out the word. "What about Casey? Is she all right?"

"Who is Casey?" Gage asked.

"Their daughter. My niece. She was with them. Is she all right? Did whoever do this kill her, too?"

Gage felt as if someone had reached into his chest and grabbed his heart and squeezed. "You're sure she was with them? How old is Casey?"

"She's five. And yes, I'm sure she was with them. You didn't see her?"

"No." He squeezed his eyes shut, trying to bring his memory of the scene at the camp into focus. No child's toys scattered about. Sleeping bags and tote box in the tent. Some clothing—maybe something pink, but at the time he had assumed it belonged to the woman. Women wore pink. But now that he thought about it again, the T-shirt had been a little on the small side for Angela Hood. "You're sure your niece was with her parents on this trip? Maybe they left her with friends or a relative."

"They wouldn't do that. Or if they did, I would know about it. If they needed someone to watch Casey, I would do it." Her voice rose, pinched with agitation. "What's happened to her?"

"I promise I'll find out. I have to go now, but I'll call you back as soon as I know something."

Fighting a sick feeling in his stomach, he hit the speed dial for Travis again, even as he started the SUV. "Those two murder victims up here?" he said as soon as Travis answered. "They had a kid with them. We've got a missing little girl."

Chapter Two

Maya Renfro gripped the steering wheel of her Volkswagen Beetle so hard her fingers ached, and depressed the accelerator until she was doing eighty. The roads were dry and clear and if highway patrol stopped her, she'd give them Deputy Gage Walker's number and tell them to take it up with him. Her sister was dead and her niece was missing, and every movement felt as if Maya were swimming through quicksand.

This had to be a bad dream. Real life couldn't be this horrible, could it?

But of course it could. You didn't teach high school for four years without seeing a little of that awfulness—kids kicked out of the house while they were still in their teens, colleagues who died of cancer, budget cuts that sliced into the most meaningful programs.

But life that bad had never happened to Maya before. It shouldn't happen to Angela—or to Casey.

She fought back tears and gripped the steering wheel even harder. She had to keep it together. When she got to Eagle Mountain, she had to be there for Casey.

The cop on the other end of the line—Gage Walker—

hadn't even known Casey existed. How was that possible? Angela and Greg never traveled anywhere without a whole carload of kid gear. Not to mention both their phones were full of pictures of Casey, from newborn right up through her fifth birthday party two months ago.

Maya had been at that party. She had brought a tiara for Casey to wear and the little girl had been thrilled. The screen saver on Maya's phone was a picture taken at the party, of her and Maya grinning for the camera.

Casey had to be okay. She had to be.

As soon as the news of Angela's death really began to hit her, Maya had tried to call the cop—Gage—again. The call had gone straight to voice mail. Instead of leaving what would probably have been a hysterical message, she left an aide in charge of her sixth period class, let her principal know she was leaving and why, and rushed home to throw a few things in her car and head for Eagle Mountain.

By the time Deputy Walker had called her back to tell her Casey was missing and they were making every effort to find her, Maya was already speeding toward Eagle Mountain. She didn't know much about the town—it was in western Colorado, apparently located in a beautiful area that attracted lots of tourists. Angela and Greg had raved about the place, both so excited over the mining claims they had bought and their plans for the property. "If this works out, we're thinking of moving to Eagle Mountain," Angela had said at dinner the night before their trip.

"You should come with us," Greg said as he passed

Maya a bowl of steamed broccoli. "You could get a teaching job there, I bet."

"You really want to live in a small town?" Maya was incredulous. "Why?" Small towns, by definition, were small, which to her meant limited opportunities, limited entertainment options and maybe even limited thinking. "You have everything you could ever want here in Denver."

"Eagle Mountain is the perfect place to raise kids," Angela said. "If we're going to relocate, now's a good time, before Casey has really settled into school."

Maya wasn't so sure about that. Wouldn't kids get bored way out here in the middle of so much *nature*? Everywhere she looked she saw endless fields, soaring mountains, colorful rocks, rushing streams and vast blue sky—but not many people or buildings. What did people out here do for excitement and entertainment?

How was a five-year-old girl going to survive alone out in all this emptiness?

By the time she turned onto Eagle Mountain's main street, she was exhausted from grief and strain, her stomach in knots with worry over Casey, and in no mood to deal with any slow-talking, easygoing backwater cop, which was the only kind she expected to encounter here. After all, if a man had any real talent and ambition, wouldn't he opt to go someplace with a little more action?

The first person to acknowledge her when she walked through the door of the Rayford County Sheriff's Department was a white-haired woman who wore purple-framed glasses and earrings shaped like pink flamingos. "May I help you?" she asked, eyes sharp, expression all business.

"My name is Maya Renfro. I'm looking for a Deputy Walker."

Any hardness melted from the woman's face. She jumped up and moved toward Maya, hand extended. "You're the sister. We've been expecting you. I'm so sorry for your loss. Such a tragedy." She ushered Maya to a small office down a short hallway. "You must be worn out. Everyone is out looking for your niece, but I'll call and let Gage know you're here. I'm Adelaide, by the way. I'll get you some tea. Or would you rather have coffee?"

"I just want to speak to Deputy Walker."

"Of course. I'll get him here as soon as I can."

Then Maya was alone in the office, a claustrophobic cube of a room with barely enough space for a desk and one visitor's chair. She sat and studied the walls, which were filled with several framed commendations and half a dozen photographs, all featuring a tall, good-looking man with thick brown hair and the weathered face of an outdoorsman. In one picture, he knelt beside a mountain stream, cradling a colorful fish and grinning at the camera. In another, he supported the head of a trophy elk, golden aspens in the background. In a third photograph, he posed with another officer, both of them in uniform and holding rifles.

"That's Gage and his brother, Travis." Adelaide spoke from behind Maya. She set a cup on the edge of the desk. "I brought you some tea," she said. "I know you said you didn't want anything, but after such a long drive, you look like you could use something."

"Tea is fine." Maya picked up the cup and sat stiffly upright in the chair. "So Gage and Travis are both law enforcement officers?"

"Travis is the county sheriff," Adelaide said. "He's out with the others. We're all just sick about this. Things like this just don't happen in Eagle Mountain."

"They happen everywhere, Addie. You know that. We're not special."

The man who moved into the room past Addie was tall and rangy, his khaki uniform streaked with dirt, his face creased with exhaustion. "Gage Walker," he said, extending his hand to Maya. "I'm sorry I wasn't here to meet you."

"I told her you were out looking for her niece," Adelaide said.

"We've got everybody in the county with any kind of experience in the woods out there looking for her," Gage said. The chair behind the desk creaked under his weight as he settled into it, and the office seemed more claustrophobic than ever with his oversized, very masculine presence. Adelaide returned to the front office, leaving them alone.

Gage didn't say anything for a moment, his eyes fixed on Maya, his expression unreadable. "Why are you looking at me that way?" she asked, setting the teacup on the desk.

He shook his head, as if coming out of a daze. "You said you're a teacher?"

"Yes. I teach high school English at Centennial High School."

Gage shook his head again. "None of my teachers ever looked like you."

She stiffened. "What is that supposed to mean?"

"Well, for one thing, none of them had blue hair."

She touched the ends of her hair, which she had dip-dyed blue only two weeks before. "I made a deal with my students. If they brought up their achievement test scores, I would dye my hair blue."

"Just not what I expected."

He wasn't what she had expected, either. He wasn't slow and dumb, but he definitely looked right at home in this rugged country.

"What happened to my sister?" she asked.

"We're still trying to get a complete picture, but it looks like your sister and her husband were in their camp when someone—probably more than one person—came up, tied their hands behind their backs and shot them."

The picture his words created in her mind was almost too horrible to bear. She forced the image away and bit the inside of her cheek to stave off tears. She couldn't break down now. She had to be strong. "They just shot them?"

"I'm sorry, yes."

"Why? And what happened to Casey?"

"We're trying to find the answers to both those questions. It's possible whoever shot your sister and brother-in-law took Casey with them. But it's also possible she ran away." He leaned toward her. "Tell me about your niece. Is she a shy child—the type who would hide from strangers?"

"Casey isn't really shy, no. But if she saw someone hurt her mother and father, of course she'd be afraid. And having a bunch of people she didn't know stomping around the woods looking for her would probably frighten her even more." She had a clear picture of the little girl, hiding behind a big rock or tree, watching all the commotion around her and too afraid to come out. "I want to go look for her. She knows me. She won't hide from me."

He nodded. "That makes sense. I'll take you up to the camp, but I can't allow you to go wandering around in the woods on your own. The terrain is rough and it's getting dark. Even the trained searchers will have to pack it in soon and wait until morning."

"Maybe she's close to the camp and she'll see me and come to me." Maya stood. "Let's go now. I don't want to waste another minute."

Gage rose also and motioned toward the door. "After you. My cruiser is parked out front."

The black-and-white SUV sported the requisite light bar on top and the legend, Rayford County Sheriff's Department, on the door. Gage walked around and opened the passenger door, then leaned in and scooped an armful of papers, file folders, gloves, a flashlight and who knew what else off the front seat. "Welcome to my mobile office," he said, holding the door wide for her.

She climbed in, studying the tablet computer mounted to face the driver, the radio and the shotgun in a holder beside her seat. Gage buckled his seat belt and started the engine. "You said your sister and her husband had just bought the property they were camping on?" he asked as he pulled out into the street.

"Yes. They closed on the purchase last week and wanted to spend some time up there, enjoying the scenery." She choked on the last word. Angela wouldn't be enjoying anything anymore.

"So they bought the property to have a place to camp? Or did they plan to build a house up there?"

"Not a house, no. They bought up a bunch of old mining claims, with plans to reopen the mines."

"Interesting choice." He turned onto the highway, leaving the town behind. "Most of those old mines haven't been worked in fifty or sixty years or more. Even then, most of them never earned much. Though I guess some people do still dig around in them as a hobby."

"This wasn't a hobby. Greg is—was—an engineer. He's developed new techniques he thinks will make those old mines profitable again. He wanted to do a demonstration project here, and use that to sell his equipment to others."

"That sounds like it could end up being pretty lucrative," Gage said. "Did he have competitors? Anyone who might have killed him to get his ideas or to stop him from implementing them?"

"No! That's crazy. He doesn't know people like that. And he had patents on all the equipment he had designed. People don't kill other people over things like that. If they wanted his ideas, they could have bought him out—or tried to."

"So he never mentioned having been threatened by anyone?" Gage asked.

"No. And Angela would have told me if he had. She wasn't one to hide her emotions from me. And if either one of them had thought they were in any danger at all, they never would have brought Casey up here."

"Can you think of any reason someone would have killed them?" Gage asked. "Something in their pasts, maybe?"

"No." She shook her head, fresh tears flowing in spite of her efforts to hold them back. "They were quiet, ordinary people." She blotted the tears with her fingers and angled toward him. "Maybe they stumbled on drug activity—a meth lab or something like that—and were murdered because of it."

"It's possible," Gage said. "And we'll look into it. But most of the meth labs have moved to Mexico these days." He slowed as they approached a bank of lights—headlights, work lights, even flashlights bobbed about in the woods on either side of the road.

"This is where they were killed?" Maya asked, staring at the confusion of lights and people—and lots and lots of trees and rocks and dirt. This was the place Angela had gushed about as being so beautiful?

"Yes." Gage shut off the engine. "Stay with me," he said. "If you go wandering off around here, you could end up falling down an abandoned mine shaft or stepping off a cliff."

"Those things could have happened to Casey," she

said, climbing out of the SUV and following him down the side of the road.

"Hey, Gage."

"Hi, Gage."

"Thought you'd packed it in for the night?"

Various people greeted the deputy as they passed. An older man with a crooked nose and bushy eyebrows approached. "Deputy Walker, what are you doing about the press?" he asked.

"I'm not really concerned about the press right now, Larry," Gage said. He turned to Maya. "Maya Renfro, this is Eagle Mountain's mayor, Larry Rowe."

"Ms. Renfro." The mayor nodded solemnly. "I'm very sorry for your loss." He turned to Gage. "Now, about the press. Something like this could reflect very badly on the town if it isn't handled properly."

"Not now, mayor." Gage pushed past him, only to be waylaid a few yards farther on by a petite woman with a large red hound on a leash. "Did you get anything?" Gage asked her.

"I'm sorry, no." The woman stopped and leaned down to pat the dog. "Daisy picked up the scent from the shirt you gave me, but after about a hundred yards, she lost it. I marked the path for you. And we can try again tomorrow if you like. Right now, Daisy is just tired and frustrated."

Daisy stared up at them with mournful brown eyes, then let out a low moan and scratched at one floppy ear with her hind foot.

"Thanks for trying, Lorna," Gage said. He patted Daisy. "Give her a biscuit from me."

Maya spotted Greg and Angela's SUV and faltered. The vehicle was surrounded by a cordon of yellow-and-black tape, and more tape marked a path from the vehicle into the woods. "Is that your sister and her husband's car?" Gage asked.

"Yes."

He took her arm. "Come on. I'm going to take you into their camp, ask you to identify some things. Their bodies have already been taken away. Can you do that for me?"

"Yes." They were just things. She wouldn't think about them in relation to death.

"Step where I step," Gage said. "Don't get off the path or touch anything." He led the way through a section of tape.

"That's their tent," she said as they approached the blue dome tent. "They bought it a couple of years ago, to replace an old one our parents gave them."

"All right." Gage led her to the tent and pulled back the flap. "Take a look inside and tell me if you see anything unusual—anything that doesn't belong to your sister, her husband or Casey."

He swept the beam of the flashlight over the contents of the tent—sleeping bags, backpack, clothing, Angela's purse. Maya covered her mouth with her hand when she spotted the purse and shook her head, swallowing hard against the sob that threatened to escape.

Gage dropped the tent flap and straightened, playing the beam of the light around and behind the tent. Pink tape fluttered from a slender metal stake behind the tent. "This is where Lorna and her dog picked up the scent," he said, guiding Maya over to the stake. "Don't walk in the path, but walk beside it. Call your niece. If she's near enough, she might recognize your voice and come to you."

Maya stared at him, still numb. "Calling her isn't going to help," she said. "We have to look for her."

"Call her. She might hear you. Identify yourself and if she's hiding, she might come out."

Maya shook her head, the tears flowing freely now. "You don't understand," she said. "I could call all night and it wouldn't make any difference. Casey wouldn't hear me. She's deaf."

Chapter Three

Gage stared at Maya. "Your niece is deaf and you're just now telling me?" he asked.

"I'm sorry! I was in shock. And it's not like I think of Casey as my deaf niece. She's just my niece. Being deaf is part of her, the way having brown hair is part of her."

"This is a little more significant than her hair color."

"I said I'm sorry." She stared into the surrounding darkness, looking, he was sure, for the little girl. Gage stared, too, his stomach knotting as the difficulty of their task sank in. Simply getting within earshot of Casey Hood wasn't going to be enough. They were going to have to get her in their sights, and then somehow persuade her that they were friendly and wanted to help her. All of that required light, which meant waiting until tomorrow to continue the search.

He touched Maya's shoulder. "Come on," he said. "Let's go."

She stared at him, eyes wide, red rimmed from crying. She didn't look quite as young as she had when she had first walked into his office. The blue-tipped hair and dangling earrings had him thinking she was a teenager then. He saw the maturity in her eyes now, and the desperate struggle to keep hope alive. "We can't just leave her out there all night—alone," she said.

"We're going to have someone here all night," he said. "I'll have them build a fire and keep it going. Maybe Casey will see it."

"I should be the one waiting," she said.

"No. You should go back to your hotel room and try to get some sleep." She started to argue, but he cut her off. "We're going to need you in the morning. Once it's light out here and we can see, we're going to need you close in case someone spots Casey. She'll recognize you and want to come to you."

She looked out into the darkness again. "Do you really think she's all right?"

"We haven't found evidence to the contrary," he said. "No signs of struggle, no other signs of blood at the scene. I think she got away from the killers." Whoever shot Angela and Greg Hood might have taken the child with them, but that didn't make sense to him. The parents' deaths had been cold and efficient—for whatever reason, someone had wanted them eliminated. Why then burden yourself with a five-year-old child? "I think Casey saw what was happening, became frightened and ran away. Tomorrow, we're going to find her." He touched her shoulder again. "Come on. I'll take you back to your hotel."

"I don't have a hotel room. I mean, I didn't call and make a reservation. I didn't even think of it."

"Then we'll find you one. Come on."

She made one last glance into the darkness beyond the camp, then followed Gage to his SUV. "I'm going to speak to the sheriff," he said. "I'll be right back."

He found Travis with a group of search and rescue volunteers who were packing up to head back to town. "I got some more information about the little girl we're looking for," Gage told them. "Seems she's deaf. So shouting her name isn't going to do any good. We'll need to make eye contact."

"I know a little American Sign Language," one of the SAR volunteers, a middle-aged woman, said.

"That might come in handy," Gage said. "Can you come back to help with the search tomorrow?"

"I'll be here."

They said good-night. Travis waited until he and Gage were alone before he spoke. "Does the sister have any idea what the Hoods were doing up here that got them killed?" he asked.

Gage glanced back toward his SUV. He could see the shadowed figure of Maya as she sat in the passenger seat. "Greg Hood was an engineer who had developed some new equipment he thought could make these old mines profitable. He purchased these old claims to create a kind of demonstration project. He and his wife and the kid were camping up here, checking out their new acquisition."

"Any enemies, threats, anything like that?" Travis asked.

"She says no, and she thinks she would know. Sounds like she and the sister were close."

"All right. Maybe we'll turn up something when we

have a chance to go over the evidence from the scene. And I'm going to talk to Ed Roberts."

Gage thought of the old man who was as close as Eagle Mountain came to a hermit. He lived in an apartment above the hardware store, but spent most of his time working an old gold mining claim in the area. "Is his claim around here?" he asked.

"Behind this property." Travis gestured toward the north.

"You think he might have seen or heard something?"

Travis's expression grew more grim. "And he's a registered sex offender."

Gage stared. He knew the department received regular updates from the sex offender registry, but he didn't remember Roberts's name being on there. Maybe it dated from before his time with the department. Now he felt a little sick to his stomach. "Did he molest some kid or something?"

"He was convicted of exposing himself to women— flashing them. It happened years ago, in another state, but still…"

"Yeah," Gage said. "Still worth questioning him."

"In the meantime," Travis said, "we'll have someone up here overnight and we'll start the search again at first light."

"That little kid must be scared to death, out there in the dark by herself," Gage said.

"At least if she's scared, it means she's still alive," Travis said. He clapped his brother on the shoulder. "Go home. Try to get some rest. Pray that in the morning we get lucky."

"I'm going to find a place for Maya to stay. I'll probably pick her up in the morning and bring her up here with me. She's the person the kid is most liable to run to on sight."

"Good idea."

Maya sat hunched in the front seat, hugging herself. "I should have started the engine so you could get warm," he said, turning the key in the ignition. "Even in summer, it can get chilly up here at night."

"I keep thinking about Casey, cold and alone out there in the dark," she said.

"Most of the time, with little kids like this, they get tired and lie down somewhere," Gage said. "We're hoping she'll see the fire at camp and come back there. A husband-and-wife team with the search and rescue squad have volunteered to stay there. They've got kids of their own, so they shouldn't be too scary to Casey."

"If she comes to them, you'll call me." It wasn't a question.

"Of course," Gage said. "As soon as we hear anything."

They drove back toward town in silence. Full darkness had descended like a cloak, the sky a sweep of black in the windshield. When he had a cell signal, Gage pulled out his phone and made a call. "Hello?" The woman on the other end of the line sounded cautious, and maybe a little annoyed.

"Paige, this is Gage Walker. Sorry to bother you so late, but I've got a lady here who needs a room for the night—probably several nights. She's the aunt of the little girl we're searching for."

"I heard about that," Paige said. "Poor thing. And I do have a room. It's my smallest one, but I doubt she'll care about that."

"Great. I'm going to take her to get something to eat, then we'll stop by."

"Sure thing, Deputy."

"When was the last time you ate?" he asked Maya as they neared town.

"I had a sandwich at lunch," she said. "That seems like days ago."

"And now it's almost ten. I know you probably don't feel like eating, but you should. And I'm starving. Let me buy you dinner, then I'll take you over to the Bear's Den."

"The Bear's Den?"

"It's a bed-and-breakfast. You should get along great with the woman who runs it."

"Why do you say that?"

He glanced at her, but it was too dark for him to read her expression. "The hair, the VW bug, the English degree—trust me, the two of you will get along great."

"Why do I get the feeling that's not exactly a compliment?"

"It's not an insult," he said.

"Then what is it?"

He searched for the right words—words that weren't going to offend her, that would convey what he really meant. "You stand out from the crowd around here," he said. "That's not a bad thing."

"You mean the blue hair," she said.

"The blue hair. The attitude."

"You think I have an attitude?" Her voice rose and she leaned toward him.

Gage bit back a groan. Yes, she had an attitude— a "don't mess with me" vibe that shone through the grief and fatigue. "I didn't say it was a bad attitude," he said. "And hey, maybe I'm full of it. Ignore everything I said."

"You're not the kind of man a woman ignores, Deputy."

The words jolted him. Was she flirting with him? But when he glanced her way, she was facing forward again, what he could see of her expression betraying nothing.

Mo's Pub was the only place open this late, so Gage drove there. When they walked in the waitress showed them to a booth. "Any word on that lost little girl?" she asked as she distributed menus.

"Not yet," Gage said.

"Tony was up there all afternoon with the search and rescue crew, and we're all praying y'all find her soon. Poor little baby. She must be scared to death up there on her own."

"This is Casey's aunt, Maya Renfro," Gage said. "This is Sasha Simpson."

"You poor thing." Sasha patted Maya's shoulder. "You must be worried sick. They're gonna find her, I'm sure of it. They won't stop looking until they do."

"Thanks." Maya looked a little dazed as Sasha hurried away to wait on another table. "She sounded really worried—and she doesn't even know me or Casey."

"She has two little girls of her own," Gage said.

"And that's the way people are around here. Everybody knows everybody and while it's not exactly family, it's something like it."

"I can see how that would be appealing," she said. "But a little claustrophobic at times, too. Sometimes I like not knowing anything about my neighbors."

Sasha returned and took their orders. Maya ordered a salad, which he expected she wouldn't eat, but she was drinking her soft drink, so that was something. "So what do you do in Denver besides teach English?" he asked.

"I do poetry slams."

Again, not what he would have expected. "That's where people get up and perform poetry they've written, right?"

"Exactly." She didn't even try to hide her surprise.

"We may be a little out of the way here in Eagle Mountain, but we're not completely backward," he said.

"Have you ever been to a poetry slam?" she asked.

"No. But then, I can't say I've ever cared much for poetry. Probably comes from having to memorize 'O Captain! My Captain!' when I was in fourth grade."

"My poetry isn't like that."

"I kind of figured."

She fell silent and Gage focused on his food as soon as Sasha had placed the dishes on the table. When he looked up again, Maya was staring at him. "I'd like to see Angela," she said softly.

He should have seen that coming. "I can arrange that. Maybe late tomorrow." He leaned toward her. "Is there someone else you should call to be here with you? Another sibling? Your parents?"

"I spoke to my parents after I talked to you," she said. "They live in Arizona. My mom isn't in good health and traveling is hard for her. And there's nothing they can do. I told them they should stay put until we know more. And there aren't any other siblings."

"Okay." So she had to bear this all by herself. He would do what he could to ease the burden for her.

"What about you?" she asked. "I know you have a brother—the sheriff. Any other brothers and sisters?"

"I have a sister. She's a graduate student at CSU. Our parents have a ranch just outside of town."

She speared a cherry tomato on her fork. "A ranch as in cows?"

"And horses. The Walking W Ranch has been in operation since 1942. My great-grandparents started it."

"So do you, like, ride and rope and all that stuff?" she asked.

He suppressed a grin. "All that stuff."

"That explains the belt buckle."

He glanced down at the large silver-and-gold buckle, which he had won as State Junior Champion Bronc Rider in high school. "I was riding horses years before I learned to ride a bicycle," he said. "And I still help out with fall roundup."

She shook her head. "Our lives are so different we could be from two different countries."

"We're probably not that different," he said. "I've found that people behave pretty much the same wherever they're from."

"Well, I'm from the city and I have no desire to ride a horse. And I hope you won't take this wrong, but I thought my sister was crazy when she said she and Greg were thinking about moving here."

"You told me they bought the mining claims for a demonstration project, not to live on."

"That's right. But they were talking about finding a place here in town. They had fallen in love with Eagle Mountain. I don't know why."

"You might be surprised," Gage said. "I've heard from other people that the place has a way of growing on you."

"I just want to find my niece and go home." She looked all in, her eyes still red and puffy from crying, her shoulders slumped.

Gage pushed aside his plate. "You must be exhausted," he said. "Let's get out of here. I'll take you to your car at the sheriff's office and you can follow me to the B and B."

Fifteen minutes later, they parked at the curb in front of the Victorian home Paige Riddell had converted into a bed-and-breakfast. The light over the front door came on and Paige stepped out. "I'm Paige," she said, coming forward to take Maya's bag. "You've had a pretty miserable day, I imagine, so I won't prolong it, but I will say how sorry I am for your loss."

"Thank you." Maya gave Paige a long look. "Gage said I would like you—that he thought we'd have a lot in common."

"That depends," Paige said. "Some folks around

here think of me as the local tree-hugging rabble-rouser, but I don't take that as an insult."

"Then yeah, I think we'll get along fine," Maya said.

"Let me show you to your room." Paige put an arm around Maya and ushered her into the house. In the doorway, she stopped and glanced over her shoulder at Gage. "Don't leave yet," she mouthed, then went into the house with Maya.

Gage moved to the porch swing to the right of the door and sat, letting the calm of the night seep into him. Only one or two lights shone in the houses that lined the street, not enough to dim the stars overhead. He thought of the little girl in the woods and hoped she was where she could see those stars, and that maybe, seeing them, she wouldn't feel so alone.

The door opened and Paige stepped out. "I got her settled in," she said. "Grief can be so exhausting. I hope she's able to get some sleep."

"I'll come by and pick her up in the morning and take her up to the campsite," he said. "We're hoping her niece will see her and come to her. I found out tonight that the little girl is deaf, so she wouldn't hear us calling for her."

Paige sat in a wicker armchair adjacent to the swing. "I can't even imagine how worried Maya is. I don't even know this kid and it upsets me to think of her out there."

Gage stifled a yawn. "Is there something you wanted to talk to me about?" he asked.

"Yes. I wanted to tell you I saw that couple—Maya's

sister and her husband—the day before yesterday. And the little girl. She was with them. Adorable child."

Gage sat up straight, fatigue receding. "Where was this?"

"Some of us from Eagle Mountain Conservation went up to Eagle Mountain Resort—you know, those mining claims Henry Hake wanted to develop?"

Gage nodded. Eagle Mountain Conservation had succeeded in getting an injunction to stop the development three years ago. "You saw the Hood family up there?"

"They were unloading camping gear from a white SUV parked on the side of the road. I guess they were camping on one of the claims near Hake's property."

"They bought the claim and I guess a few others in the area," Gage said. "But what were you doing on Henry Hake's land? It's private property."

Paige frowned at him, a scowl that had intimidated more than one overzealous logger, trash-throwing tourist or anyone else who attracted the wrath of the EMC. "We weren't on his land. There's a public easement along the edge of the property. It's a historic trail that's been in use since the 1920s. We established that in court, and Hake and his partners had to take down a fence they had erected blocking access. It was part of the injunction order that stopped the development."

"So you went up there to hike the trail?"

"We had heard complaints that the fence was back up, so we went to check," she said.

"And was it up?"

"Yes. With a big iron gate across it. Our lawyers

have already filed a complaint with the county commissioners. We tried getting in touch with Hake, but didn't have any luck."

"He's been missing for almost a month now," Gage said. "No one has heard anything from him, and every trail we've followed up on has gone cold."

"A man like that probably has plenty of enemies," Paige said. "And he hung around with some nasty people. Maybe that former bodyguard of his did him in."

"Maybe so, though we haven't found evidence of that." Hake's one-time bodyguard had died in a struggle with Travis when he had kidnapped the woman who was now Travis's fiancée. Three years previously, the same man had murdered Andy Stenson, a young lawyer in town who had also worked for Hake.

Paige leaned toward Gage. "It looked to me like work has been done up there on Hake's property," she said. "There's a lot of tire tracks, and maybe even a new building or two."

"I'll see if I can find out anything," Gage said. "Maybe someone working up there saw or heard something related to the Hoods' killing." He stood. "Thanks for letting me know. I'll see you and Maya in the morning."

"I'm hoping she'll get a good night's sleep," Paige said. "And that tomorrow we find her niece safe."

"We all hope that." He returned to his SUV and headed toward the house he rented on the edge of town, but he had traveled less than a block when his cell phone rang. "Gage, this is Al Dawson, over at the high school."

"Sure, Al." Gage glanced at the clock on his dash. Ten minutes until midnight. "What's up?"

"I came in to do the floors here in the gym, but found the lock on the door is broken. Somebody bashed it in."

"Did you go inside?" Gage asked, looking for a place to turn around.

"No. When I saw the damage to the door, I figured I'd better call you. It looks like we've got another break-in."

"I'll be right there, Al. Don't go in."

"I won't. What's going on, Gage?" Al asked. "Travis was out here just this morning to take a report on some items that were stolen from the chemistry lab. This used to be such a peaceful town—now we've got crime all over the place."

"I don't know, Al," Gage said. "But I'll be right there." Ordinarily, a random burglary wouldn't seem that unusual, but two burglaries in one week was enough to rate a headline in the local paper. Add in a double murder and Gage had to ask what the heck was going on.

Chapter Four

On his way to the high school, Gage called Travis. "Didn't you respond to the high school this morning about a break-in?" he asked when his brother answered the phone.

"Yesterday morning," Travis said. "It's already this morning."

"Sorry to wake you," Gage said. "But I just got a call from Al Dawson, the janitor over there. He says the gym door has been tampered with."

"All the doors were fine when I was out there," Travis said. "The thief got into the lab through a broken window."

"Al thinks somebody broke into the gym. I'm on my way out there."

"I'll meet you."

Al was waiting by his truck when Gage pulled into the lot at the high school. Security lights cast a jaundiced glow over the scene. Whoever had attacked the door to the gymnasium hadn't bothered with subtlety. They had bashed in the area around the lock with a sledgehammer or iron bar. "Is this the only door that's been damaged?" Gage asked.

"I think so," Al, a thin man in his sixties, said. "I took a look around while I was waiting for you and I didn't see anything else."

"You don't have any security cameras focused on this area, do you?" Gage asked.

Al frowned. "We're a rural school district. Our budget doesn't run to security cameras."

"All right." Gage took out a pair of gloves and pulled them on. "I'll check things inside. You wait here."

But before he could open the door, Travis pulled up. Gage waited for his brother to join them. Travis greeted them, then surveyed the door. "They obviously didn't care about hiding the damage," he said. "Same thing with the science lab yesterday—smash and grab."

"What did they take from the lab?" Gage asked.

"Science equipment—some test tubes and flasks, reagents and a Bunsen burner," Travis said.

"You think it was kids making drugs?" Al asked.

"Kids or adults," Travis said. "We're keeping our eyes open."

"I was just about to take a look inside," Gage said.

"I'll come with you." Travis pulled on a pair of gloves and followed Gage inside, both men careful to keep to one side, out of what they judged was the direct path of entry. Later, a crime scene team would investigate and gather what evidence they could. "I don't hold out much hope of getting good prints," Gage said as he flipped the light switch. Banks of floodlights lit up the wood-floored space. Basketball hoops hung from

the ceiling at either end of the gym, and metal bleach-
ers lined the far wall.

"Doesn't look like they did any damage in here,"
Gage said, surveying the empty room.

"Let's get Al in here and see if he sees anything out
of place." Travis walked back the way he and Gage had
come. A minute later, he returned with the janitor. "Do
you see anything missing, Al?"

The janitor scratched his head. "I don't see anything—
then again, I wouldn't necessarily know. You need to get
one of the coaches over here for that."

Gage checked the time. Almost one in the morning.
"For now, we'll seal off the area and get one of the reserve officers over here to babysit the scene until the
crime scene guys can make it over. What time do the
coaches show up?"

"Seven thirty or so, usually," Al said. He frowned
across the silent gym. "I guess this means I won't be
doing the floors in here tonight."

"No one comes in here without an escort from the
sheriff's department," Gage said.

They went outside again and while Travis pulled
crime scene tape from his SUV, Gage called in a reserve officer to stand guard and made notes about Al's
statement. "I'll swing back here early to talk to the
coaches," he said.

Thirty minutes later, he and Travis walked back to
their cars, prepared to leave. "Did you get Ms. Renfro
taken care of?" Travis asked.

"She's over at the Bear's Den," Gage said. "I told
her I would pick her up and take her back to the camp

in the morning. She wants to help search for her niece, and I think it's probably a good idea. The little girl will recognize her, plus Maya can communicate with her in sign language." He glanced over his shoulder at the high school. "I guess I'll swing by here first, see if I can get anything useful from the coach."

Travis clapped him on the shoulder. "Let me know what you find. I'll see you later at camp."

Gage opened the driver's-side door of his SUV. "And to think just yesterday I was complaining about being bored," he said. "That's what I get for opening my big mouth."

MAYA LAY AWAKE much of the night, alternately weeping and praying, terrified of what might be happening to Casey, unable to accept she would never see her sister again.

When the clock showed 6:00 a.m., she got out of bed and took a shower, then did her makeup and ventured downstairs. When she walked into the dining room, which was painted a cheery apple green, Paige gestured toward a buffet, on which sat a large coffee urn and plates of muffins. "Help yourself," she said. "The other guests haven't come down yet, but I knew you'd want an early start."

Maya filled a coffee cup and stirred in cream and sugar. "I don't guess you've heard anything from Gage?" she asked.

"I'm sorry, no," Paige said. "I'm sure he would have called you if they had found anything."

Maya dropped into one of the chairs at the dining

table. Paige sat opposite her. "I know it's hard," Paige said. "But don't give up hope. Everyone available is looking for your niece—and we've done this before. Two summers ago, a little boy got lost when his family was hiking and they found him the next day, a little cold and scared, but safe."

Maya wrapped both hands around the sky-blue mug decorated with little fleurs-de-lis. "I keep telling myself that we'll find Casey today. I wish I was up there right now, helping to look for her."

"It's still too dark out to see much," Paige said. "And do you even know how to get there?"

"Gage took me there last night." She sipped her coffee. "And I can follow directions, if someone tells me which way to go."

"You might as well wait for Gage," Paige said. "He should be here soon."

"He probably has plenty to do besides babysitting me," Maya said.

"He probably does," Paige said. "But that's the kind of guy he is—a real gentleman. I know it's an old-fashioned word, but it's true. He really cares about people. It's what makes him good at his job."

Maya shifted in her chair, curiosity warring with embarrassment. Curiosity won. "Are you and Gage involved?" she asked.

Paige laughed. "Oh my goodness, no. What made you think that?"

"I know you went down to talk to him after you showed me to my room. I just thought…" She shrugged.

"No. Gage and I are not involved." Paige pinched

off a bite of muffin. "Neither one of us is interested in getting serious," she said. "It's easier."

"I know what you mean," Maya said. "I'm not seeing anyone right now, either." Though she couldn't help thinking how nice it would be to have someone she could lean on. She pushed the thought away. She had been standing on her own two feet for plenty of years—no reason to stop now. "How did you end up in Eagle Mountain?" she asked.

"I came here on vacation and fell in love with the place," Paige said.

"Where did you live before?" Maya asked.

"Portland, Oregon."

"This is certainly different from Portland," Maya said.

"Different was what I needed at the time. I was coming off a painful divorce, and both my parents had died in the three years prior to that. I had a little money my aunt had left me, so I used it to buy this place and fix it up." She shrugged. "At the time, I thought maybe I would stay a few years then move on, but I got involved in life here and I love running the B and B. It's a good fit all around."

"I think small-town life would bore me after a while," Maya said.

"There's plenty to do here if you know where to look," Paige said. "Maybe not as many choices as in the city and we're low on anything resembling the club scene, but I've made a lot of friends here. I care about this place and it feels like home."

The doorbell chimed and Paige scraped back her chair. "That's probably Gage."

Maya told herself her heart beat faster because she was hoping for news from Gage about her niece, but she had to admit to the thrill of attraction that ran through her when the sheriff's deputy stepped into the dining room. "Good morning," he said, and nodded and touched the brim of his hat.

The courtliness of the gesture moved her. He looked tired, and there was a heaviness about his eyes that heightened her own sadness. "Did you get any sleep last night?" she asked.

"A little." He accepted a cup of coffee from Paige, and pulled out the chair next to Maya. "I had a late call. Break-in at the high school."

"Kids?" Paige asked.

"Maybe." Gage sipped his coffee.

Maya thought of the students in her classes—a mixed bunch of good and bad. "I guess even little towns like this aren't immune to that kind of thing," she said.

"Kids get bored and in trouble everywhere," he said. "Though we like to think in Eagle Mountain there's a little less trouble for them to find. No gangs, anyway. Drugs are always a concern, but there's not as much of it here. And people in smaller communities get involved—if they see a kid up to something, they don't hesitate to call it in."

"I guess being nosy has its upside," Maya said.

"It can." He helped himself to a muffin. "We can go whenever you're ready."

"Let me grab my backpack."

She waited until they were on their way before she

asked the question that had been foremost in her mind all morning. "Have you heard anything from the other searchers?" she asked.

"I'm sorry. No." He glanced at her, then back at the road. "Have you thought about where Casey might have gone if she ran away? Let's go with the theory that she saw what happened to her parents and ran, scared. Is there anything in particular that she's attracted to? Is she drawn to water? Would she hide in a cave, or would she avoid that?"

"I think a cave would frighten her. I don't think she cares about water, one way or another." She frowned, trying to think past her exhaustion and fear. "I mean, she's five years old. She's a sweet, innocent girl who's never known danger for a minute in her life. Seeing her parents killed—" She shook her head. "She must be terrified."

"We haven't found any indication that the people who killed your sister and her husband harmed Casey," Gage said. "Hold on to that hope."

She nodded. "I will. I'm hoping Casey spent the night hiding, and once she sees me, she'll come out."

"That's what we're hoping, too."

"You were right—I do like Paige. And she vouched for you as a good guy."

"Were you worried I was otherwise?"

"No, but it's always good to have someone verify my first impression."

"Glad I passed the test. Though I can't say I'm all that comfortable knowing you two have been discussing my merits and flaws."

"Ha! As if men don't do the same with women."

"I promise, I haven't discussed you with anyone."

Under other circumstances, that admission might have disappointed her, Maya told herself. But there were bigger things at stake right now. "What's the plan for this morning?" she asked.

"I think you should hang around the main camp. If any of the search team spot Casey, or any signs of her, they can contact the base and we'll get you to that location."

That sounded like a lot of sitting around and waiting for other people to find Casey—not what she had in mind. "What are you going to do?" she asked.

"I want to take a look at the property adjacent to the place your sister and her husband owned. A few years back, a developer bought it and had plans to build a big resort, but he ran afoul of local environmentalists. The property is supposed to be vacant, but Paige told me last night she was up there a few days ago and it looked as if someone had been working there. If I can find whoever that was, maybe they saw something that will lead us to your sister's killer. Or maybe someone there has seen Casey."

"Or maybe this mysterious person *is* the killer." Maya wrapped her arms across her stomach to ward off a chill.

"Maybe." Gage looked grim. "It's something I need to find out."

"I want to come with you," Maya said. "If there are other people working there, it makes sense that Casey would have headed in that direction."

"I don't know what I'm going to walk into," Gage said. "I can't risk putting you in danger."

"I don't care about that." When he gave her a questioning look, she set her jaw. "No offense, Deputy, but I'll do almost anything to save my niece. That's more important to me than anything else right now."

"And if I order you to stay away?" he asked.

"Then you would have a fight on your hands," she said. "And when it comes to people I love, I'm not afraid to fight dirty."

"The scary thing about that," Gage said, "is that I absolutely believe you."

"Why is that scary?"

"Let's just say, I never met a teacher like you. I'm still making up my mind whether I like that or not."

"You don't have to like it. Just don't stand in the way of me taking care of my niece."

"I won't stand in your way," he said. "Unless you're in mine. But I think we're on the same side in this matter. Just respect that I have a job to do. I want to find your niece as much as you do, but I also need to find your sister's killer. I think we can do both."

"Are you going to take me with you this morning or not?"

She waited a long, tense moment for him to answer. If she had to, she would go to his brother, the sheriff. Or she would get the press on her side—there was bound to be a reporter at the site, surely.

"All right, you can come with me," he said. "But if I sense anything dangerous, I'm taking you right back to camp—no arguments."

"All right." That would have to do—for now. Maya had meant it when she told Gage she would do anything to protect her niece. Anything at all.

Chapter Five

Gage wasn't used to people pushing back against decisions he made as an officer of the law, and his first instinct with Maya had been to shut her down. But he had heard the determination in her voice and seen the grief in her eyes, and recognized a fight he couldn't win. He didn't really expect to run into any danger on Henry Hake's land, and if they did, he was confident he could protect them both.

He parked behind Travis's SUV and the sheriff walked out to meet them. "The first group of searchers just went out," he reported. "Lorna has her dog with her, and a couple of other people say they know a little sign language, so if they see Casey, they can try to communicate with her."

"Thank you," Maya said. She looked pale in the early morning light, and Gage read the disappointment in her eyes. She had been hoping for word of her niece when they arrived—she wanted to hear that the little girl had already been found.

Gage put a hand on her shoulder. "Wait over by the fire for me. I need to talk to the sheriff for a minute."

She nodded and moved toward the fire, a sad but determined woman. Gage didn't know if he would be as strong if he were in her position.

"What did you find out at the high school?" Travis asked, bringing Gage's attention back to work.

"I talked to the head coach. He says they're missing three gym mats, a climbing rope and some weights."

Travis's brow furrowed. "Nothing anyone could really sell, and I don't see how any of those things could be used to manufacture drugs."

"Right," Gage said. "So maybe it's just kids?"

"Maybe," Travis said. "Though when kids vandalize a school, they do it to make a mess—graffiti, tearing things up. This doesn't feel like that."

"Yeah," Gage agreed. "It feels like someone went in there looking for some specific items, grabbed them and got out."

"More than one person, probably," Travis said. "That's a lot to carry. Those mats are bulky and the weights are heavy."

"The mats are bright blue," Gage said. "We'll keep our eyes open around town—maybe we'll spot them."

"In the meantime, we'll put extra patrols around the school," Travis said.

"I want to take a look on Henry Hake's property this morning," Gage said. "It's close enough Casey might have wandered over there. She might be hiding out in one of the buildings."

"It's a long way for a kid that little to walk," Travis said.

"Only about a mile cross-country," Gage said. "That

little boy who was lost last year was over three miles away from the place his folks had last seen him."

"Give it a go then. Has the mayor talked to you yet?"

Gage frowned. "He stopped me last night, blathering something about the press and the town looking bad."

Travis nodded. "He called me first thing this morning. He's worried Eagle Mountain is getting a reputation as an unsafe town."

"What did you tell him?"

"I told him we were doing our best to find the person responsible for these murders and I didn't think anyone else was in danger."

"What did he expect?" Gage asked. "That you could wave a magic wand and make all the bad things disappear?"

"He's just doing his job, looking out for the town's reputation," Travis said.

"Then he needs to leave us alone to do our jobs."

"If he bothers you again, send him to me," Travis said. "Do you have anything new on this case?"

"Paige told me she was up here with members of her environmental group two days ago and she saw the Hoods unloading their car," Gage said. "The group had heard a report that the public trail that runs alongside Hake's property had been blocked and they came to check it out. Paige said someone had put up a gate and the addition was recent. You haven't heard anything about any new activity at the resort, have you?"

"No," Travis said. "Henry Hake is still missing, and as far as I know, the injunction against his development is still in effect."

"I'll check it out. I'm taking Maya with me." Gage didn't mention she had insisted on coming with him.

"I got a preliminary report this morning on the Hood murders," Travis said. "They were both shot with a nine millimeter. Close range, one bullet each. Killer took the spent shells with him."

"So they weren't killed during a struggle," Gage said.

"I don't think they had a chance. I think they were jumped, tied up and shot. Two, but I'm guessing three people to do the job."

"And where was the little girl while all this was going on?" Gage asked.

"The coroner puts the time of death around 9:00 p.m., so maybe she was in the tent, asleep."

"The killers would have gone in looking for her."

"Not if they didn't know she existed. Or maybe she woke up when her parents were attacked and crawled out of the tent and ran."

"Tents don't have back doors," Gage pointed out.

"No, but this one had a good-sized tear in the back window screen. A frightened little kid could have gotten out that way."

"And the killers didn't hear her?"

"Not if they were busy with the parents."

Gage nodded. The scenario made sense. "We need to find her today," he said. "She's got to be cold and hungry and scared." If she wasn't lying at the bottom of a ravine or drowned in a creek. He didn't have to say those things out loud—he knew Travis was thinking them, too.

"Check out Hake's. Take others with you if you need to."

"I think Maya and I will have a look by ourselves first," he said. "As it is, if word gets out we were over there, we're liable to hear from Hake's lawyers. They've got the place fenced off like a fortress."

"Let them complain about us searching for a missing child and see what kind of PR that gets them," Travis said.

Gage found Maya standing by the campfire with Mellie Sanger, half of the couple who had stayed at the site overnight. Maya turned toward Gage as he approached, the hope in her eyes like a stab to his heart. "Mellie was telling me they stayed up most of the night and didn't hear or see anything," she said. "I don't see how Casey could have just vanished."

"She's probably afraid and hiding," Gage said. "As she gets hungrier, she'll want to come out." That was all the hope he had to give her right now.

"Good luck." Mellie took both Maya's hands in hers. "George and I will come back tonight if we need to, but we really hope we don't need to."

"Thank you both, so much."

"Are you ready to go?" Gage asked.

"Yes." She hitched her backpack up on her shoulder. "Which way?"

He led the way east, toward the land Henry Hake had wanted to develop. There was no defined trail, and the going was rough, over uneven ground littered with fallen tree branches and small boulders. They crossed a small stream, and then another, then descended into a steep ravine. Gage could hear Maya breathing hard as they climbed back out of the ravine, but she kept up with him and didn't complain. A few hundred yards on, they stopped to drink some water. "How could a little girl have crossed all that?" Maya asked.

"People lost in the wilderness do incredible things," he said. "The little boy we found last year—the one who had wandered away from his parents while the family was out for a hike—ended up three miles away from the trail, in a place he would have had to cross three streams and climbed a small mountain to get to."

"How did they ever find him?" she asked.

"Persistence and luck," Gage said. "Lorna's dog, Daisy, found the trail initially, then a group of volunteers spread out to search a hundred yards on either side of the trail. They found him asleep in the hollow made by an uprooted tree trunk. If they hadn't been looking for him, they might have walked right by and never seen him."

"I don't know if that story makes me more hopeful or more horrified," she said. She stuffed her water bottle back in her pack. "I've been staring at the ground all morning, hoping to see a little footprint or some pink thread—Casey loves pink, and almost all her clothes are pink. I want so badly to see some sign of her that I'm half-afraid I'll start imagining things."

"I'm watching, too," Gage said. "Maybe we'll spot something soon." Or maybe they wouldn't. He kept talking about the little boy they had found last summer to encourage her, but he didn't mention the three or four other people over the years who had become lost and were never found—or whose bodies were found months or years later.

After a half hour of walking, they came to an eight-foot-tall chain-link fence topped with razor wire, hedge roses poking through the wire and blocking the view beyond. "Whoa!" Maya stopped and stared up at the barrier. "What is this doing out here? It looks like something the government would build around an airport—or a prison."

"The landowner, Henry Hake, doesn't like trespassers." Gage wrapped his fingers around the chain link and tugged. Still taut and solid as the day it had been built four years ago, and the thorny roses added to the barrier. "He planned to build an exclusive—expensive—resort community up here. I guess this fence was supposed to keep out the riffraff."

"Casey couldn't have gotten over this," Maya said.

"No, but it's possible she found a break in the fence, or a place where an animal had dug under. Plus, a public trail crosses one corner of the property and it's not supposed to be fenced off." He scanned the terrain on either side of the fence. "Come on," he said, pointing north. "Let's see if we can find a way in."

MAYA TRUDGED ALONG behind Gage, trying hard not to freak out over the idea of Casey being lost out here. Everywhere she looked, she faced another hazard: tree stumps to trip over, holes to fall into, rocks to stumble on. And what about wild animals? Surely there were bears and mountain lions and no telling what else out here that might view a five-year-old girl as a tasty

snack. She shuddered and pushed the thought aside.
A child couldn't just vanish this way. She had to be
somewhere.

"Look here."

Her heart jumped in her chest at Gage's words, and
she hurried to catch up to him. He stood alongside the
fence, pointing to a depression in the ground. "This
looks like a place some animal has been going under
the wire," he said.

Maya frowned at the muddy hole. "You think Casey
went under there?"

"She might have. She would fit, wouldn't she?"

"Yes, but why would she get down in the mud like
that?"

"If she saw people or saw a building on the other
side, she might risk it," he said.

She turned to look through the fence. The rose
hedge was less dense here, but she didn't see anything
but trees at first. Then she spotted what looked like the
corner of a building. "If she did go in there, how are we
going to follow?" she asked. "I can't fit through that
hole, and I know you can't."

"We should be getting to the public trail soon."

Another ten minutes of walking took them to the
end of the fence—and to a large iron gate blocking a
well-worn trail. "That looks new," Maya said, studying the fresh-looking concrete around the gateposts.

"It is new," Gage said. "And it's against the law to
block a public trail." He looked around, as if searching for something.

"What are you looking for?" Maya asked.

"Something to break that padlock."

The padlock was large and heavy. "I don't think a rock is going to do it," she said.

"No." He drew the gun from the holster at his hip. "Stand back."

"You're not going to sho—" But apparently, he was. The blast echoed through the woods and Maya covered her ears and closed her eyes. When she opened them again, the lock lay shattered on the ground.

Gage pushed open the gate. "Stay behind me, and if we meet anyone, I'll do the talking."

She resisted the urge to roll her eyes at him. She got that he was used to being in charge, but he ought to have figured out by now that she didn't like being ordered around. She forgot her annoyance as she moved farther away from the gate into what looked like a long-abandoned ghost town. The remains of paved streets showed between patches of grass and even small trees that grew up through the asphalt. A few windowless concrete buildings crouched alongside crumbling concrete foundations or stakes topped with faded plastic ribbons that fluttered in the breeze.

Maya moved up alongside Gage. "What is this place?" she asked, keeping her voice low. "It's creepy."

"It was going to be an exclusive resort, with luxury homes, a country club and a golf course."

"Why wasn't it built?"

"Paige and a group of like-minded citizens got together and filed a lawsuit to stop the building. They convinced a judge that this was a fragile environmental zone that wouldn't support that kind of development. The judge agreed."

"Do you agree?" she asked.

He glanced at her. "I do. But I can't say leaving it like this is much better. It's an eyesore." He led the way across one of the crumbling streets, toward a row of three curved ducts jutting up from the ground.

"What are those?" she asked.

"Probably air vents for underground storage, or possibly machinery—a power plant or something. They could even be venting gasses from an old mine."

"I don't think Casey could climb down in them, and I don't see a door."

"No." He walked on, to a windowless building made of concrete blocks. The single steel door was fastened with a heavy bolt, with a lock through the bolt.

Maya put her ear to the door and listened, but heard only the thump of her own pulse. She stepped back and looked at Gage. "Are you going to shoot this lock off, too?"

"No reason to," he said.

They moved on, the only sound the crunch of their shoes on gravel. No birds sang; no machinery hummed. She rubbed her arms against a sudden chill. "I don't like it here," she said. "I think we should leave."

"Something feels off to me, too," he said. "But I'd like to stay long enough to figure out what that is."

"What do you think—"

But before she could complete the question, gunfire exploded from their left and something slammed her down hard into the dirt.

Chapter Six

Gage threw himself onto Maya, forcing her down into the dirt, as bullets cut the air around them. He wrapped his arms around her and rolled with her, into the shadow of the concrete building, on the side away from the shooting. He strained to listen for sounds of movement, but heard nothing but his own and Maya's labored breathing. Slowly, he eased off her, but kept one hand on her back. "Stay down," he said, his mouth close to her ear.

"Did someone just shoot at us?" she whispered, and he heard the terror behind the words.

He didn't answer her question, but instead rose to a crouching position and drew his gun. "I'm going to take a look," he said. "Stay down."

"I'm not moving."

He moved to the corner of the building, staying low, and hazarded a look around the side. No bullets came his way. But in the distance, an engine roared to life, and a car door slammed. He glanced back at Maya, who still lay huddled against the building. "Don't move," he ordered. Then, keeping to the cover of trees and rocks, he started toward what he estimated had been the shooter's location. The spot, in a growth of scrubby bushes on a rise above where he and Maya had been standing, offered cover and a good view of much of the proposed resort development. Whoever had shot at them could have been up here watching them since they had stepped through the gate. Gage shooting off the lock had given them plenty of notice that they had visitors.

He examined the ground around the area. A few scuff marks indicated someone might have been there recently, but he couldn't see any distinct shoe prints. He moved a few feet away from the bushes, to a wide, flat area with the faint indentation of tire tracks. These were probably from the vehicle he had heard. There was only one way they could have driven from here, and it led toward the road. They were probably out there and long gone by now—but he would make sure.

He hurried back down the slope, where he found Maya seated, her back against the door of the building. She looked up at his approach. "Did you find anything?"

He shook his head and held his hand out to her. "Let's head back by the road," he said.

"Can you call for help?" she asked.

"No cell signal up here," he said. He pulled her to her feet. She straightened and brushed dirt from her shirt and jeans.

"Why would someone shoot at us?" she asked. "Is it the same person who shot Angela and Greg? Do you think they have Casey?"

"I don't know. Maybe whoever put that gate up doesn't like trespassers."

They reached the front entrance to the property. Maya stuck close to him, tensed and looking around her. But Gage didn't see a sign of anyone. They set out walking down the road and five minutes later, he recognized Travis's SUV headed toward them.

The vehicle slowed and stopped as it pulled alongside them. "I heard gunshots," Travis said.

"The first shot you heard was me, shooting the lock off an illegal gate across the public trail that runs along one side of Henry Hake's property," Gage said. "The second set of blasts was somebody shooting at us. Did you pass any other vehicles on your way up here?"

"No." Travis jerked his head toward the passenger side of the SUV. "Get in."

Gage held the door for Maya as she climbed into the back seat. "There's some bottled water back there if you want some," Travis said.

Maya took a bottle of water from the box on the back floorboard and handed another to Gage. "Have you heard anything about Casey?" she asked.

"I'm sorry, no," Travis said. He turned the SUV around. "I'm going to take you back to camp and you can talk to the searchers, hear from them what they've seen. Then Gage and I will come back up here."

"I looked around, but whoever took the shots at us didn't leave much behind," Gage said. "Some faint tire tracks. No bullet casings or shoe prints."

"Maybe you missed something," Travis said. "What were you doing when they shot at you?"

"We were walking around," Gage said. "Looking for anywhere a little kid might hide or might be drawn to."

"Did you find anything?" Travis asked.

"No." He glanced back at Maya. "She's out there. I know it," he said. "We're going to keep looking."

She nodded, but the sadness in her eyes was a weight on his heart.

CASEY'S CHEST HURT. Every breath felt like something was cutting her on the inside. But she was too afraid to stop running—too afraid of the men with the guns. The men who had hurt Mommy and Daddy.

Her eyes filled with tears, making the world look blurry. She tripped on something and fell hard. Pain shot up her knee and she cried out. She had fallen so often since she had run from the camp the night before last. Was it really that long ago?

She crawled to the base of a big tree and huddled there, tears streaming, nose running. She wiped at it with her sleeve. *Stop crying!* she ordered herself. Crying didn't help anything. She closed her eyes and tried to think.

Aunt Maya was here. Casey had seen her, with the big policeman. Or maybe not a policeman. What did you call them when they wore brown instead of blue? A sheriff? A sheriff's deputy had come to their school once. He was Alexa Steiner's dad, and he had told them when they were in trouble, they should find a law officer to tell.

Was Aunt Maya in trouble? Was that why she was with the deputy? Or maybe he was protecting her from the men with guns. He had pushed her down when the men began firing.

And Casey had run. She had to run. She was so afraid of the men—more afraid than she had ever been. So afraid it made her shake, just to remember what had happened. She didn't want to remember. She drew her knees up to her chest and rested her head on them and shut her eyes. If only she could go to sleep and wake up to find this was all just a nightmare.

But she had slept last night—curled on the ground under a tree that looked a lot like this one—and when she woke in the morning, she had been scared all over again, not knowing where she was. Everything here looked so different from home—so many rocks and trees, and the big open sky and no buildings or streets or people she knew.

"Mommy," she whispered.

But her mommy wasn't going to come back again. Neither was her daddy. She had seen them lying on the ground, bleeding, and the bad men looking in the tent—the tent that Casey had crawled out of when the men had grabbed Mommy and Daddy and tied them up. Then she had run again, as long and as far as she could. She had to stay away from those bad men.

Her tummy growled and she raised her head again. She was so hungry. She had drank water from a stream last night and again this morning, but she didn't have anything to eat. When she saw those buildings, she thought she might find some food, but instead, the bad men had come and scared her away.

A bird screeched overhead. She looked up and followed its flight, into some bushes with red things on them. She stood and went over to the bushes. The red things were berries—raspberries. She picked one and popped it into her mouth. It was little but so sweet! Hurrying, she picked more, stuffing the berries into her mouth until her hands were covered with the bright red juice and her arms were covered in scratches from the prickly bushes. She moved from bush to bush, eating as many of the berries as she could find. They tasted so good—better even than candy.

When she had eaten all the berries she could hold, she walked until she came to another stream. She crouched down beside it and washed her hands and face, then scooped up water and drank. Now that she had eaten, she was so tired. But she couldn't just lie down out here in the open—the bad men might see her.

She looked around and saw a hole in the middle of a clump of bushes—like the door to a little cave. She went over to it and looked inside, at the smooth carpet of leaves. It was just big enough for her to curl up. She crawled in and did so, and thought of a storybook Aunt Maya had read to her and the picture in the book of the little squirrel curled up in its nest. She was like that squirrel, safe in this nest. She closed her eyes and thought of the squirrel, and of Aunt Maya. Maybe she would come soon and take her away—far away from the bad men.

DOZENS OF PEOPLE were swarming around Angela and Greg's camp when Maya returned with Gage and Travis. The blue tent still stood to one side of the fire pit, with the clothing and sleeping bags inside. Maya wondered if they had left everything in place as a landmark for Casey to hone in on. She was surprised to see Paige there, standing with a pretty brunette. Gage's brother, Travis, moved ahead of Gage and Maya and kissed the brunette on the cheek and she smiled up at him—the kind of smile only people in love exchange.

"Lacy and I brought some food up for the volunteers," Paige said. "And we thought we would help with the search if we could."

"I saw the gate over the trail, over by Hake's place," Gage told her. "I shot the lock off, so it's open now."

"The county says they'll order Henry Hake to take it down," Paige said. "As soon as they find him. I tried calling his office, but nobody answers."

"Somebody must be running the business in his absence," Gage said.

"Where is he?" Maya asked. "Why can't you get in touch with him?"

"No one knows where he is," Paige said. "He's been missing about a month now." She held out her hands, palms up. "He just disappeared."

"We've been looking for him," Travis said. "But if someone doesn't want to be found, it can be tough."

Paige took Maya's hand and squeezed it gently. "How are you doing?" she asked.

"I'm hanging in there." Later, when this was all over and Casey was safe, she would probably collapse, but so far, she was managing to stay strong thanks in part to all of these people—none of whom she had known before yesterday—who were helping to search for Casey.

"We're going to find her," Paige said. "You can't give up hope."

Maya nodded. Hope was the only thing keeping her upright.

"We need to warn everyone to stay away from Hake's place," Travis said.

"Why is that?" Lacy asked.

"Somebody took a shot at Maya and Gage when they were over there just now," Travis said. "As soon as I spread the word here, he and I are headed back over there to investigate."

"Be careful," Lacy said, then bit her lip, as if wishing she could take back the words, but Travis only squeezed her hand.

"I always am," he said.

"Someone shot at you?" Paige stared at Maya, open-mouthed. "Who?"

"That's what we're going to find out." Gage turned to Maya. "You'll be okay here while I'm gone? If you want to go back to town, I can find someone to take you."

"No. I want to stay here. I can't leave until we find Casey."

"And here come more recruits," Paige said, looking over Maya's shoulder.

She turned to see two men approaching. The shorter of the two was also the more muscular, with bulging biceps and a shaved head. His companion was tall and lean, with a weathered face and short blond hair.

"We closed up early and came to see what we could do to help," the blond said.

"Maya Renfro, this is Brock Ryan." Gage indicated the blond. "And Wade Tomlinson. They own Eagle Mountain Outdoors."

"We brought our climbing gear in the truck," Brock said. "Just in case."

"Speaking of climbing gear," Gage said. "Somebody stole a climbing rope from the high school last night. Any ideas who would take something like that?"

"Maybe some kid who was into climbing?" Wade answered. "Good gear is expensive—more than most high schoolers can manage without help from Mom and Dad."

"Can you think of anybody we should question?" Travis asked. "Maybe a kid who's been hanging around your shop?"

The two men exchanged looks. "I can't think of anyone," Wade said.

"Me, neither," Brock agreed.

"Go talk to Tony with search and rescue," Travis said. "He's coordinating the volunteers." He turned to Maya. "I think you should stay here in camp, so people know where to find you if they have any sightings. Casey is probably afraid, and she might not readily come to anyone but you."

She nodded. "Of course I'll stay. I—"

"What's the reason for all this commotion? I've had people tramping all over my land all day and I want it stopped now!"

They all swiveled to see a big, hawk-nosed man with

a striking cascade of snow-white hair past his shoulders stalking toward them. He halted in front of Travis, though he practically vibrated with rage. "These people don't have any right to come on my property. What are you going to do to stop them?"

"Hello, Ed," Travis said. "I went over to your place yesterday to talk to you, but you weren't home. Or at least, you didn't answer the door."

"Just because somebody comes to my door doesn't mean I have to talk to them," Ed said. "What are you going to do about all these people invading my privacy?"

"We're looking for a little girl." Travis took one of the flyers that had been distributed to all the volunteers from his pocket and unfolded it. "Have you seen her?"

The flyer featured a picture of Casey—the one from her birthday party that Maya had given to Gage to use. She watched the old man's face as he studied the picture. After a few seconds, he thrust the flyer at Travis. "I don't have anything to do with kids," he said.

"Except that young woman in the park in Pennsylvania," Travis said.

Ed's face flushed a dark red. "That was fifteen years ago. I leave everybody alone and I ask that they do the same for me."

"So you didn't see a young couple—this little girl's parents—over here next to your property and wonder what they were up to?" Gage asked.

Ed glanced around at the crowd. Everyone within earshot had stopped to listen to the exchange. "I saw some people over there," he said. "But I didn't talk to them. I keep to my property and they kept to theirs."

"Did you see anyone else over here?" Travis asked. "Any strangers? Or did you hear anything? Any shouting or gunfire?"

"No."

"Would you have called us if you had?" Gage asked.

Ed just scowled at them.

"Do you own a gun?" Travis asked.

"A man has a right to protect himself."

"We're going to want to search your place," Travis said. "The one in town and the one up here."

"You can't do that without a warrant."

"Then we'll get one."

"You have no right! I'll—"

But a shout and the sound of running feet interrupted him. A young man and woman raced up, breathless. "We found this," the man said, and held up a small pink sock.

Maya swayed, fighting dizziness, her gaze fixed on the bright pink sock—so tiny in the man's hand. A strong arm came around her shoulders, and she looked up into Gage's concerned face. "Do you recognize it?" he asked.

"I…I don't know. I mean, it's so small. But Casey loves pink. She always wears it."

"Where did you find it?" Travis asked.

"It was caught in some bushes, beside a creek down

there." He pointed to the north. "I marked the spot with my bandanna."

Gage's hand tightened on Maya's shoulder. "That's on your land, isn't it, Ed?"

Chapter Seven

Gage's arm around Maya's shoulders was warm and strong, holding her up and silently encouraging her to hang on. "I'm all right," she said, her eyes fixed on the sock. As long as she looked at it, she didn't have to look at the old man. Had he hurt Casey? But then, why come into camp and call attention to himself this way?

"I'm going to get someone to take you back to town," Gage said. "I know the waiting is hard, but we want to do this right, get the warrant, make sure we don't overlook anything."

She nodded, and her shoulders straightened. "All right."

"We'll take her back with us," Paige said.

"We'll do our best to distract you," Lacy said.

"Is that okay with you?" Gage looked her in the eye. That steady gaze made her feel stronger—calmer.

She nodded. "Just call me as soon as you know anything."

"I promise I will."

Paige drove the three women back to the Bear's Den. "Make yourselves comfortable," she said, showing them into a sun-filled room on the top floor of the three-story house. "I'm going to open a bottle of wine."

Lacy settled on the end of the sofa, legs curled beneath her. "One thing you should know about the Walker men," she said. "They don't give up. They'll find your niece."

Maya sat at the opposite end of the sofa. "I know they're trying," she said.

Paige joined them, a bottle of white wine in one hand, three glasses in another. She handed them each a glass and poured the wine. "What we really want to know is all about you," she said. "Who is Maya Renfro?" She sat in an armchair across from the sofa. "You're not just Casey's aunt or Angela's sister. It's too easy to put people in those little boxes."

"Paige doesn't like boxes." Lacy sipped her wine and smiled.

"I'm guessing someone with blue hair doesn't like boxes, either," Paige said.

Maya sipped the wine, buying time to think. "Maybe I just haven't found the box I fit in yet," she said. "I'm single. I'm from Denver, and I teach school."

"I'm studying to be a teacher," Lacy said. "I'm hoping to go into elementary education."

"I teach high school. Teenagers are practically a different species. Challenging, but I think that's why I like them." She fingered the blue ends of her hair. "I never would have done this if my students hadn't challenged me. I told them if they improved their test scores, I'd dye my hair. They did, so here I am. But I'm thinking of keeping it. It unsettles some people and I'm enough of a rebel I like it." She shrugged.

"What else?" Paige prompted. "Any hobbies? What do you do for fun?"

"I perform at poetry slams."

"One of the women I knew in prison did that," Lacy said. "Not slams, really—but she wrote poetry and performed it for the rest of us. She was really good."

Maya stared at the pretty brunette over the rim of her wineglass. "Prison? Did you work there?"

Lacy laughed. "No, I was in prison for three years. I was wrongfully convicted of killing my boss."

"Travis Walker got her out," Paige said. "He proved she was innocent, then found the real killer."

"I take it you and the sheriff are involved?" Maya asked.

Lacy's smile made her seem to glow from within. "We are. And believe me, I'm the last person I'd ever expect to fall for a lawman."

"The Walker brothers are both easy on the eyes," Paige observed. "And even though Gage says he's not interested in a relationship, I'll bet he would change his mind for the right woman."

Maya felt both women's eyes on her, even as she studied the contents of her glass. "He's been very kind," she said, determined not to betray the flutter in her stomach when she thought of Gage.

"They come from one of the town's founding families." Paige leaned over to tip more wine into Maya's glass. "You should see if Gage will take you to visit the Walking W Ranch some time."

"It's pretty spectacular," Lacy said. "Like something out of a Ralph Lauren ad—big log ranch house, rolling pastures right up to the base of the mountains."

"Why did they go into law enforcement instead of running the family ranch?" Maya asked.

"Oh, they're still involved with the ranch," Lacy said.

"Their dad is only in his early fifties, and he's one of those men who seem like he could still be going strong for another thirty years," Paige said.

"Travis has never come right out and said so, but he really wants to help people," Lacy said. "It's important to him to make a difference in his hometown."

"He could make a difference in a city, too," Maya said.

"Sure he could. But this is home."

"Don't take this the wrong way," Maya said. "But I never understood that—feeling so tied to a place. I mean, isn't it kind of, well, limiting to live in the same place all your life, with the same people who know everything about you?"

"I know what you mean," Lacy said. "And I used to feel the same way—especially when I was a teenager, dying to get away." She shrugged. "But then I went away, and I couldn't wait to get back. There's something special about this place. It kind of gets under your skin."

"But you're from here," Maya said. "I've never lived anywhere but the city."

"That was me, before I came here," Paige said. "I always thought a small place would limit me, but it's the opposite. I've really grown here and been able to try new things. In the city, there is always someone who has done what you're thinking about doing and they've done it better. That can be inspiring, but it can also be paralyzing. Here, if you want to do something, you may be the first to try it—like starting an environmental group, which is what I did."

"Or a poetry slam." Lacy nudged Maya with her toe. "We don't have that here."

"I'm not sure Eagle Mountain is ready for poetry slams," Maya said. She didn't bother to point out that she wouldn't be staying in town long enough to get involved in anything. As soon as Casey was safe, Maya would need to take her back home. They would need time to heal in the place that was familiar to them both.

"How long do you think it will take them to get the warrant to search that man's place?" she asked, unable to tear her thoughts away from that topic for long.

"I don't know," Lacy said. "Probably not long. The judges know Travis and he has a good reputation. They trust his judgment, and he wouldn't ask for the warrant without proof."

"I had no idea old Ed had a record," Paige said. "I just thought he was a grouchy old hermit—another town character."

"Maybe that's all he is," Lacy said. "He may not have anything to do with any of this."

"If he does, Travis and Gage will find out," Paige said.

Lacy set her empty wineglass on a side table. "I wish there was more we could do to help," she said.

"You're doing a lot," Maya said. "Being with me like this now—it helps so much." It struck her that back home, she didn't have friends like this. She was on good terms with the other teachers she worked with, but for so many years, Angela had been her best friend. Paige and Lacy couldn't replace her sister, but being with them helped her feel less alone.

As soon as Maya was safely away, Gage rejoined Travis, who was just ending a phone call. "I've got the request for the warrant started," he said. "While we wait, we can go back to Hake's place and have a better look around."

They rode together, in Travis's vehicle. "Do you really think Ed had anything to do with the Hoods' deaths?" Gage asked as Travis drove.

"He never struck me as the particularly violent type, but who knows? Maybe he thought Greg Hood was a threat to his own mining operation. Or maybe he's a sicko who wanted the little girl."

"Yeah." You didn't have to be in law enforcement for very long, or in a big city, to learn that people did horrible things to each other all the time—even people you would never suspect.

When they reached the fence that marked the boundary of Henry Hake's land, Travis parked at the road and he and Gage walked into the development, past the fading sign announcing the resort, with its rendering of soaring log chalets and cobblestone drives set amidst golf greens, swimming pools and stables. The picture bore little resemblance to the crumbling concrete and weeds around them. "Where were you when the shots were fired?" Travis asked.

"Over here." Gage led the way to the cinder block

building. Travis tried the door, which was still padlocked. "The shots came from over there." Gage indicated the slope that rose up from the building. "That little bunch of trees in there."

The two brothers walked up the slope, and Travis knelt to study the rocky ground beneath the scrub oaks. Then he examined the faint tire tracks Gage pointed out. "We'll take a casting, but I'm not holding out hope we'll find anything," Travis said. He looked around the empty landscape. "Whoever this is, they know how to clean up after themselves, not leave any trace." He stood. "I want to take a look around at the rest of the place."

The afternoon sun beat down on what was left of the streets, and a breeze that carried a hint of a chill fluttered the flags on the wooden stakes that marked lot lines and building sites that had long been abandoned. "This place gives me the creeps on a normal day," Gage said as he and Travis walked past rusting rebar jutting up from half-finished foundations. "But this afternoon, even before the shots were fired, it felt like someone was watching us. Maya felt it, too."

"I don't sense that now," Travis said.

"No. I think whoever was here earlier is long gone."

"I need to take a look at the official plat of this place and see if these air vents are on there," Travis said, as he and Gage drew alongside the arching metal structures.

"That's a good idea," Gage said. "I don't hear any fans or machinery or anything."

They walked around the side of the structure, down

a steep slope and around to the back. Travis walked slowly, studying the ground, then pushed aside the arching branches of a stunted juniper to reveal a metal door. Unlike the other structures around them, the door looked new, the dark green paint—the same shade as the juniper branches—bright and fresh.

Travis tried the door. It didn't budge. He straightened and let the branch fall back into place. "Without a warrant, we can't get in."

Gage scratched his ear. "If we said we heard something, and we thought Casey might be trapped in there…"

Travis sent him a look. The *don't be an idiot, little brother* look that Gage had known all his life. Then he led the way back up the incline, to the mouth of the air vents. He cupped his hands around his mouth and shouted down one of the tubes. "Hello! Casey, are you in there?"

Gage held his breath, straining to make out any noise coming from the vents, but the only sound was the wind flapping the plastic flags on a row of survey stakes. "She can't hear us," he said, remembering.

"I know," Travis said. "But I was hoping maybe vibrations…" He let the words trail off and the two walked on, to the highest point of the property, overlooking Dakota Ridge and the valley below. Gage squinted against a glare from something downslope that was reflecting light back into his eyes. "What's that down there?" he asked, pointing toward the brightness. He squinted more, focusing in, gaze traveling from the starburst of glare along a dark shadow, and something smooth like glass. Honed in and fully alert, he touched Travis's arm. "Is that a car down there?"

Travis stared also. "Maybe. Let me get my binoculars from the cruiser."

While Gage waited for Travis to return, he studied the slope above what he was now sure was a car. The terrain was mostly bare rock, though maybe that was a broken branch there and a dislodged boulder a little farther up—evidence that the vehicle had careened down that slope before coming to rest in a knot of trees. There was an old mining road up there, used now by hikers and a few of the more daredevil four-wheelers. He couldn't imagine who would be fool enough to drive a full-sized automobile up there.

Travis returned at a trot, panting a little as he stopped and lifted the binoculars to his eyes. "It's a car," he said. "Or rather, some kind of SUV. Black. I can't see anyone in it, but we'll have EMS on standby just in case."

"Can you read the plate?" Gage asked.

Travis's boot scraped on rock as he shifted his weight. "Yeah. And I know that number." He lowered the binoculars, a frown deepening the *V* between his eyebrows. "That car is registered to Henry Hake. We may have finally found him after all."

Chapter Eight

By the time Gage and Travis made it back to the camp, Deputy Dwight Prentice had arrived with the warrant to search Ed Roberts's property. "Call Gracy's Wreckers in Junction and tell them we've got a vehicle we need to bring up out of the canyon below Dakota Ridge," Travis told Dwight as he accepted the warrant paperwork. "And we'll need to send search and rescue over there to see if there's anyone in the vehicle."

"Off Dakota Ridge?" Dwight frowned. "Where? Who drove off there?"

"Gage and I saw the vehicle from over at Henry Hake's place," Travis said. "It's an SUV with tags registered to Hake."

"He's been missing almost a month now," Dwight said. "If he's in that vehicle, he isn't alive."

"We're not sure he's in there," Gage said. "But we have to check."

"If there's nobody alive in the wreck, we can wait until morning to retrieve it," Gage said. "But we need to find out. I want you to go over there with the search and rescue crew."

"Will do," Dwight said.

Travis was reviewing the paperwork when Lorna Munroe approached, the bloodhound, Daisy, straining at the leash. "I wanted to let you know we found a match for that little girl's sock the searchers found earlier," Lorna said. "I gave the second sock to Daisy and she followed the scent for half a mile or so along the creek before she lost it. So many people have tramped through these hills recently looking for that child that I think it's getting tough to pick out one trail from all the others."

Gage bent to scratch behind one of Daisy's long ears and she rolled her eyes up at him in a mournful look.

"We appreciate you trying," Travis said. He folded the papers and tucked them into his shirt pocket. "Come on, Gage," he said. "We'd better get going."

The brothers didn't speak on the short drive to Ed Roberts's place. Ed met them in front of what could only generously be termed a shack. The tin-roofed building was the size of a backyard storage shed, constructed of scrap lumber salvaged from old mining structures, with a single window and a door that had started as a green slab of wood and warped as it dried so that it no longer closed all the way. "We got the warrant," Travis said, and handed Ed the papers.

Ed adjusted a pair of wire-framed glasses on his nose and studied the documents. Gage had been prepared to have to argue with the old man—maybe even physically restrain him. But Ed only took off the glasses and said. "You'd better come in and get it over with."

Inside, the floor of the one-room building sloped toward the back, and the small space was crammed with an old leather recliner patched with tape, a wooden trunk that doubled as a table, a battery-operated camping lantern and packing boxes full of books, mining equipment and ore specimens. "You can look all you want," Ed said. "There's no place to hide anything here."

Gage met his brother's eyes. Ed was right—with all three of them inside, there was hardly enough room in the shack to turn around.

Travis peered into a box of books. From where Gage stood by the door, most of the titles appeared to have to do with mining or history. "Did you have any arguments with Greg Hood?" he asked.

"Who?" Ed asked.

"He's the father of the little girl who's missing," Travis said. "He and his wife own the property to the south of your place. Somebody shot them and killed them."

Ed blinked. "Was he a young man, sandy hair and expensive clothes?"

"That would be a pretty good description," Travis said. "Did you and he argue?"

"No! I talked to the man exactly once. I met up with him when I was walking my property line. Just him. We got to talking. He went on about some invention he had that was going to make all these old mines profitable again."

"So you lied earlier, when you told us you didn't have anything to do with Greg Hood," Gage said.

"We exchanged a few words, that's all. They minded their business and I minded mine."

"So the two of you didn't disagree about anything?" Gage asked. "Maybe you thought his invention was going to cut into your own profits from your mine?"

"I didn't take him seriously," Ed said. "I've met plenty of folks in my time who think they're going to buy a claim and get rich. Then they find out what hard work mining really is, and how tough it is to make it pay off, and they give up and go home. I figured this guy would be the same."

"So the two of you had a nice, pleasant conversation," Travis said.

Ed glared. "I told him the last thing I wanted was a bunch of folks with dollar signs in their eyes traipsing around up here."

"What did he say to that?" Gage asked.

"He laughed. He thought I was colorful. A character."

"That didn't make you angry, when he laughed?" Travis asked.

"I told you, he didn't matter one whit to me. I've seen his kind before. Big thinkers—not such big doers. If he wanted to play around out here with his invention, it wasn't any skin off my nose—as long as he stayed off my property."

"Did he?" Travis asked.

"As far as I know, he did."

"When was this, that you saw him?" Gage asked.

Ed considered the question. "Day before yesterday, in the afternoon."

"What about Henry Hake?" Travis asked. "Did you ever run into him?"

"He's that developer who wanted to put in that big fancy resort, right?" Ed asked.

"Yes," Travis said. "Did you ever have any conversations with him?"

"Never met the man. Never cared to. I saw him on television a couple of times, talking up the place, and I drove over there one day to look around. They had built a big fence around the land, and had No Trespassing signs every few feet. I thought they were crazy if they thought they would ever get rich people to pay a fortune to live up here. Even I don't come up here after the snow starts. The only way in is on skis or snow-shoes or on a snow machine. And the first time an avalanche comes down on one of those fancy homes he wanted to build, he'd lose his shirt in the lawsuits that would follow."

"So you haven't been over to look at the property recently?" Travis asked.

"I drive by it all the time," Ed said. "It's an eyesore now. The county ought to make them clean it up. They cut down all those trees and poured all that concrete and now it's all sitting there, a blight on the land."

"So you haven't been over there, just to look around?" Gage asked.

"I already told you, no. Those places attract the wrong kind of people."

"Who is that?" Gage asked.

"The folks who want to build the fancy houses and

the environmentalists who protest against them. I got no use for any of them."

"You don't have much use for most people," Gage said.

Ed lifted his chin. "That's right. But I didn't kill anybody, and I didn't hurt that little girl."

"We're going to take a look outside now," Travis said.

Ed followed them outside. "You want to look in my outhouse?" he asked. "Go ahead."

"Gage will take care of that," Travis said.

Gage sent his brother a look that told Travis payback was in his future. But the outhouse—a portable toilet rented from a local company—wasn't as bad as Gage might have feared, and it was definitely empty.

Next, they visited the mine adit, a timber-framed hut extending from the side of the hill. "It's a hundred feet to the main shaft," Ed said. "There aren't any lights, so if you're going to look around, I hope you brought your own illumination."

Travis unclipped a heavy-duty flashlight from his belt. "We'll be fine."

He led the way into the tunnel, Gage reluctantly following. Ed remained outside. "Let's hope the old man doesn't decide to wall us up in here," Gage grumbled.

"What made you think of that?" Travis asked.

"Just my dark imagination."

The tunnel sloped upward, rock pressing in on all sides. Before they had gone more than half the distance, they both had to hunch over to avoid scraping against the ceiling. Water ran down the center of the tunnel, making footing slippery. "I hope we don't run into any bats," Gage said. "I hear bats like these old mine tunnels."

"Shut up," Travis said, and played his light over the walls and ceiling, the light glinting on bright flecks in the gray granite.

"Is that gold?" Gage asked.

"Probably pyrite or quartz," Travis said. "Fool's gold."

Eventually, they reached the first shaft—a round hole at their feet scarcely wide enough to accommodate a man. Travis shone the light on a wooden ladder fastened to the wall of the shaft. "I think I should wait up here while you check this out," Gage said, eyeing the narrow opening. "If something goes wrong with you, I can run for help."

Travis glared at him, but pocketed his flashlight and knelt beside the shaft. "Light my way down," he said.

Gage knelt beside the shaft and shone the light into the opening. Travis climbed down, the soles of his boots ringing hollow against the wooden rungs of the ladder. Within a few minutes, he landed at the bottom of the shaft. Less than a minute later, he started back up. "There's nothing down there," he said.

Gage reached down to give him a hand up. "I'm sure Ed got a charge out of knowing that."

Travis wiped his hands on his pants. "We had to look, but I don't think that little girl is here."

The two trudged back to the cruiser. Ed was nowhere in sight, but that was fine with Gage, who had no desire to speak with the grouchy old man. He climbed into the cruiser and stared out at the lengthening shadows. "I don't like the thought of that little kid out here another night," he said.

"No." Travis started the engine. "And the longer she's missing, the lower the odds we'll find her okay."

"Maya wants to spend the night out here, in case Casey shows up. I think I should stay with her."

"All right." He turned onto the road. "Though I don't think she's going to fall for your charms as easily as some of the local women."

Gage scowled at him. "I'm not trying to charm anyone here. Maya is a nice person in a horrible situation."

"But as you have said so often before, you like women. And for some reason I can't fathom, they like you. Don't complicate an already complicated situation."

"I'm not trying to complicate anything." And he wasn't setting out to seduce Maya. Yes, he had dated a number of women in town, and maybe that had given him a certain reputation. But it wasn't a bad reputation—all the women he had dated knew he would show them a good time and keep things fun. They all enjoyed themselves and nobody got hurt.

He didn't see Maya the same way. There was nothing fun about what she was going through. He just wanted to be there to help if she needed it. He stared at the blur of scenery rolling past. "Maya is only going to be in town a little while," he said. "I'll do what I can to make that time easier on her."

And if he had regrets when it came time to say goodbye, no one had to know that except himself.

THE THREE WOMEN were starting on a second bottle of wine when the wail of a siren cut off their conversation. Maya didn't pay much attention—she was used to hearing sirens at all hours of the day and night, but apparently the sound was cause for alarm here in Eagle Mountain. "That sounds like an ambulance," Paige said, setting aside the wine.

She moved to the front window and Lacy followed. "It is an ambulance," Lacy said. "Do you think it's an accident? Or maybe someone had a heart attack?"

"Maybe."

The other two women were so concerned, Maya began to be nervous also. "Do you think they found Casey?" She stood on shaky legs. "Why didn't someone contact me? If she's hurt—"

"We don't know that yet." Paige hurried over to put her arm around Maya, even as she pulled her phone from her pocket and punched in a number. "Hello, Adelaide? This is Paige Riddell. We just heard the ambulance and wondered if you know where it's going?"

She listened for a moment, then said, "Wait a minute. I'm going to put you on speaker so Lacy and Maya can hear. They're with me. Would you mind repeating that?"

Adelaide's voice was loud and clear on the phone's speaker. "I said, Travis and Gage found Henry Hake's car in the ravine below Dakota Ridge."

"Was Henry Hake in the car?" Lacy asked.

"They don't know," Adelaide said. "They've got search and rescue out there trying to figure that out— the ambulance is headed out there on standby. Though if poor Henry's been in that car as long as he's been missing, he's past any help the EMTs can give him."

Maya sank onto the sofa once more, too shaky to stand. "We thought maybe they had found little Casey," Paige said.

"Not yet," Adelaide said. "Travis did say there was no sign of her out at Ed's place."

"Thanks, Adelaide," Paige said. "You'll let us know if you hear anything?"

"You'll probably hear from Travis or Gage before I do."

Paige ended the call and sat next to Maya. "I'm sorry it wasn't better news," she said.

Maya nodded. She was fighting hard to keep it together and not break down. She had to hold on to the hope that Casey was alive and okay, but the more time dragged on, the tougher that was to do.

The doorbell rang. Paige patted Maya's shoulder and stood. "I have to get that."

"Of course."

She left and Maya listened to her footsteps retreating down the stairs. "Would you like more wine?" Lacy asked.

Maya shook her head. "I think I've had enough." She didn't think she could drink enough to forget for one second about her lost niece or her dead sister, so why bother trying?

Then a man's voice drifted upstairs, and every nerve in her body leaped to attention. She stood and walked toward the door to the hallway, even as the man's footsteps started up the steps. "Hello, Maya," Gage said.

She studied his face, trying to read the emotion there—was he coming to bring bad news, good news or no news at all?

"We don't have any word about Casey yet. I'm sorry," he said. "But we didn't find any sign of her at Ed Roberts's place. We checked his apartment in town, too, but I really don't think she's been there."

"Thanks for letting me know." She marveled at how calm the words sounded, even as her stomach churned.

"Do you still want to go out to the camp tonight?" he asked.

"Yes."

"Then I'll take you," he said.

"You don't have to do that," she said. "I know where it is now. And I'm sure you have work to do. I'm not your full-time job."

"The sheriff wants an officer out there overnight, so I volunteered," he said.

"All right. I'll just pack a few things."

When she left, Paige and Lacy were questioning him about Henry Hake's car. In her room, Maya stuffed a backpack with a fleece pullover, hat and gloves, and another pullover that would be way too large for Casey, but would keep the girl warm if she was cold. She looked around the room but could think of nothing else useful to bring, so she hurried back upstairs. Gage met her in the hall. He didn't say anything until they were in his SUV.

"If you want to see your sister and her husband, the coroner has the bodies ready for viewing," he said quietly.

The meaning behind his words hit her like a bucket of ice water. She had kept all her energy focused on Casey, not allowing herself to think about Angela and Greg, and the fact that they had been murdered.

Gage must have read the emotions on her face. "I know it's a lot to ask," he said. "But we need you to confirm the identification."

She clenched her hands, nails biting into her palms. "I won't believe they're gone until I see." Even then, she wasn't sure the reality would ever sink in. Angela and Greg were so young. They weren't supposed to die. Not this way.

"I'll let him know we're on our way."

He made the call while she sat, numb, staring out the windows but not seeing anything. Gage touched her arm. "You need to fasten your seat belt," he said.

"Oh, sure."

He drove across town, to a white Georgian building with columns across the front and a circular drive. A low sign by the drive read McCasklin's Funeral Home. Gage drove around to the back and led the way to a side door, which was opened by a middle-aged man in a dark suit. "I'm Ronald McCasklin," he said, offering his hand. "I know this is a difficult time for you, Ms. Renfro. Please let me know if there's anything I can do to help."

Given his profession, he had probably said words similar to this many times before, but they struck Maya as sincere. "Thank you," she whispered.

"They're in viewing room one," McCasklin said to Gage.

"This way." Gage put a hand on her back and guided her down the hallway, their footsteps silent on the thick burgundy carpet.

"I thought we'd be going to a hospital or a morgue," she said, keeping her voice soft.

"We don't have either of those here," Gage said. "When the coroner needs facilities for an autopsy, he uses this place." He opened the door with the gold numeral one affixed to its center. The overhead light cast a soft golden glow over the figures lying side by side on rolling steel tables, sheets pulled up to their chins, as if they had merely stretched out for a nap.

But no one napping would be this pale or this still. Maya stopped halfway across the room, rooted in place by the sight of her sister and brother-in-law's cold, impassive faces. Whoever had worked to make them presentable had combed their hair over the worst of their injuries, but couldn't completely hide the wound over Angela's forehead. Maya put a hand over her mouth, trying—and failing—to stifle a sob.

Gage turned her into his chest and she surrendered to that calm strength. He held her while she sobbed, not saying anything—not trying to quiet her or uttering any of the awful empty platitudes people turned to in such times. He simply stood there and held her, and let her soak his uniform shirt with her tears.

Chapter Nine

Maya didn't know how long she cried, but after a while she managed to stem the tide of tears. Gage stuffed a handkerchief into her hand—not a paper tissue, but a white cotton handkerchief that smelled of starch. "Are you ready to leave?" he asked.

She nodded. "Yes." She had seen more than enough. The people lying on those tables bore a resemblance to Angela and Greg, but they weren't them. The personalities who had given life to those waxen shells were gone from this place. That was the loss she was mourning, the deaths she might never come to terms with.

Ronald met them at the door and silently pressed a plastic cup of water into Maya's hand. She nodded her thanks and let Gage lead her to the SUV. He helped her into the passenger seat and buckled her seat belt, as if she were a little child.

He said nothing, and she appreciated the silence. After a while, some of the shock began to recede. She sipped the water and stared out at the houses they drove past. "Where are we going?" she asked after a while.

"Nowhere in particular," he said. "Just driving.

Checking on the town. It's part of the job to keep an eye on things."

"So you're looking for crime?" She studied a bungalow they passed, the front yard filled with blooming flowers. "Is there a lot of that here?"

"Not really. But I'm not really looking for crime. Or not only looking for crime. I'm looking for signs of anyone in trouble. It might be a kid out after dark by himself, or a man who's locked himself out of his car. It might be papers or mail piling up at a house where I know an elderly person lives alone."

She shifted toward him. "It's like you're watching over the whole town."

"I guess you could think of it like that."

She drank the rest of the water and set the empty cup on the floorboard. "Seeing Angela and Greg that way—it was so horrible, and yet, I think I had to do it. To accept that they're really gone."

"If you hadn't done it, would you regret it?" Gage asked.

"Probably, yes."

"Then you probably made the right decision."

"Maybe. Do you have any idea who killed them?"

"Not yet. We've got someone going through the items in the tent and their SUV, hoping for a clue. And we have their phones and are looking at those records."

"What are you looking for?"

"Someone they might have talked to or arranged to meet. Anyone they might have had an argument with."

"You don't think it was an accident—a hunter's stray bullets or something like that?"

"No. Whoever killed them did so deliberately." He glanced at her. "I'm sorry. That's hard to hear."

Yes, it was. But she would rather know the truth than try to soothe herself with lies. "I can't imagine what either of them could have done to upset anyone," she said. "They both had so many friends in Denver. And they were so happy." She bit her lip, dangerously close to another flood of tears.

Gage swung the SUV back onto the town's main street. "I thought maybe we'd get some food to go and take it up to the camp," he said.

"All right." She didn't feel like eating, but he was probably hungry. He had been working most of the past two days. "You must be exhausted," she said.

"It hasn't caught up to me yet, but it will. Then I'll sleep twelve hours and be good to go again. It's like this when something big is going down."

He stopped by a café and she waited in the cruiser while he went inside. She pulled out her phone and pretended to focus on it, aware of curious eyes on her as people walked by on the sidewalk or came to the doors of adjacent businesses. Maybe some of those people felt sympathy for her, or maybe they were only curious about the woman with blue hair who was riding with the deputy, wondering if she was his latest conquest.

Gage returned to the cruiser, a large brown sack in his hand, which he stowed in the back seat. "Anything else you need before we head out of town?" he asked.

"I don't think so."

As he drove toward the highway, she angled toward him, searching for anything to distract her from her grief and worry. "Paige told me you have a reputation as the town Casanova," she said.

He glanced at her, then shifted his gaze back to the road. "Don't believe everything you hear."

"But you have dated a lot of women."

"I'm friends with a lot of women. We go out and have a good time. I don't go around being a jerk and breaking hearts."

"Okay." What had Paige said... *Gage says he's not interested in a relationship.*

"So what is it—you just don't want to be tied down, or you're afraid of getting hurt, or what?" she asked.

"You think a guy needs a reason to be single? That if he is, it means he's hurt or damaged or something?" No mistaking the annoyance in his voice.

"No. I was just curious." And it was interesting that he got so defensive.

"What about you?" he asked. "Are you seriously dating anyone?"

"No." She wasn't dating anyone at all.

"So are you afraid or hurt or something?"

"Or something." She faced forward once more.

"I'm all ears," he said.

She sighed. She had asked for this, hadn't she? And what difference did it make if she shared her sorry dating history with Gage? In another day or two, she would probably be leaving town and would never see him again. "I dated a guy for three years," she said. "About the time I was expecting him to pop the question, he told me he wanted to break up. And yeah, it hurt. And maybe it made me a little gun-shy. So I'm not blaming you for not wanting to get serious with anyone—I was just curious."

He didn't say anything, his hands rubbing up and down the steering wheel as if he were debating between polishing it and ripping it off the steering column. "I dated a woman right after I started with the department," he said. "I wasn't thinking about marrying her or anything like that, but I was really into her. She told me she didn't see a future with a law enforcement officer—the job is too hard on long-term relationships. I decided she was right."

"Just like that, you let one woman decide your future?"

She half expected a growl to accompany the glare he sent her way. "You let one guy who dumped you decided *your* future."

Touché. "Isn't that great?" she said. "We have something in common."

A heavy silence stretched between them as the road wound up above town. It narrowed and the growth of trees became thicker, the houses fewer.

"Being a deputy in a rural county like this isn't as dangerous as being a cop in the inner city, maybe," he said. "But there are risks. I know my mother worries every day about Travis and me. Lacy worries about Travis. I don't see any reason to put that burden on anyone else."

"The right woman wouldn't see it as a burden."

"Then I guess I haven't found the right woman."

He pulled onto the shoulder in front of Angela and Greg's property. A Rayford County Sheriff's Department cruiser sat in the space where their SUV had once been parked. Maya supposed the vehicle was at some sheriff's department facility now, being examined for evidence.

A tall, rangy deputy walked out to meet them. "Maya Renfro, this is Deputy Dwight Prentice," Gage introduced him.

Dwight shook her hand. "I'm sorry I don't have any new information about your niece," he said. He turned to Gage. "Search and rescue confirmed there's nobody in that car, so the wrecker will be out tomorrow mid-morning to haul it out."

Maya left the two men discussing this and moved to the fire ring, where a few coals still smoldered. Angela and Greg's tent sat to the side. Maya glanced in the door, then looked away. Empty of the clothing and sleeping bags and other things that had belonged to her sister and Greg, the tent was just another object cluttering up the landscape.

Gage joined her, carrying two camp chairs and the brown paper sack. He handed her the sack and set up the chairs, then began adding wood to the fire. "When the sun goes down up here, it gets pretty cool," he said. "We'll be glad of the fire."

Casey would be cold, she thought. Maybe she would see the fire and come to them.

She sat in one of the chairs and Gage took the other and began unpacking their dinner. He passed her a barbecue sandwich. "Try to eat something," he said. "There's chocolate pie for dessert."

Maya started to cry. The burst of tears shocked

her—she had thought she had pulled herself together. But his mention of the pie undid her.

Gage set aside the food and took her hand. "What is it?" he asked.

"Chocolate pie," she sobbed. "It was Angela's favorite."

"I'm sorry," he said. "I didn't mean to upset you."

"It's not your fault." She grabbed a paper napkin and blotted her eyes. "How could you know? And I've got to learn to cope with this. I can't fall apart every time something reminds me of her."

Gage released her hand and sat back once more. "That will take time."

She nodded and picked up the sandwich. "I'll be fine. I promise I'm not going to do this all night."

"Would it help to talk about her?" he asked. "Tell me a good memory you have."

She had so many memories of Angela—she searched for one that would give him a good picture of their relationship. "When we were in middle school, she had most of our classmates convinced that she and I were twins—our story was that she was smarter, so she had managed to skip a grade, which explained why she was ahead of me in school."

"Sounds like she was pretty persuasive."

"I thought being twins would be cool, but I was annoyed that she insisted she was smarter—even though it was probably true."

"When Travis and I were in middle school, *he* told everyone that I wasn't his real brother—that our parents adopted me when the circus came to town," Gage said.

"That wasn't very nice."

"When my mother found out, she grounded him and made him spend the first month of summer vacation scraping and painting one of our barns. By the second week, we both complained so much she made me go out and help him." He tossed another branch on the campfire. "I guess in the end, it made us closer."

"I was always grateful to have a sister who could be my friend, too," she said. She had been lucky, even if her luck had run out too soon. She wrapped her half-eaten sandwich in a napkin and set it aside. "I think I'll have some of that pie now."

The pie was excellent—densely chocolate and smooth as silk, whipped cream mounding the top. "Angela would have loved that," she said when she was done, her voice only a little shaky.

Gage leaned forward and wiped a smear of chocolate from her mouth. Such a simple gesture, yet it struck Maya as one of the sexiest things anyone had ever done for her. Was there something wrong with her, that she could feel aroused at a time like this? Or was it only a testament to how much life fought to win out over death every time? Was this just a way for her body to remind her that for all the bad things going on right now, she had to hold on to the promise of good in the future?

Their eyes met and she realized Gage was feeling it, too. She leaned closer and put her hand on his shoulders and kissed him. A gentle brush of her lips, then a harder caress, then a fierce, openmouthed kiss. A thrill raced through her and she leaned in to it, exulting in this feeling that somehow cut through the smothering blanket of grief.

He returned the kiss with a fierceness that matched her own, his hand gripping her shoulder as if to steady them both.

He pulled away first. "Whoa," he said, his voice a little hoarse.

"Yeah, whoa." She looked away, her cheeks warm, wondering what had come over her.

He leaned over to poke the fire, she suspected to give them both time to recover. But then he froze. "Did you hear that?" he whispered.

"Hear what?" She couldn't hear anything over the pounding of her heart.

He held up one hand, head cocked, staring into the darkness past the fire.

Then she heard it. A small, thin wail.

She was on her feet and racing toward the sound before she even realized what she was doing. Gage pounded after her, the beam of his flashlight cutting a path through the darkness ahead of them.

And then they saw her—the tiny, stumbling figure. Casey wailed and held out her arms. Maya scooped her up, then sank to her knees, her tears mingling with those of her niece as they clung together.

Chapter Ten

It seemed to Gage as if half the town was waiting in front of the sheriff's office when he pulled up with Maya and Casey. As soon as he had found a good cell signal, he had phoned Travis to give him the news and asked him to have the EMTs meet them. Though Casey appeared to be in good shape, considering she had spent the last forty-eight hours wandering around in the woods, he thought it would be a good idea to have her checked out, just to be sure.

The EMTs—or possibly Adelaide—must have spread the word, because despite it being after nine o'clock on a weeknight, cars crowded the street for three blocks on either side of the station, and a broadcast van from a Junction television news program was set up in the middle of the street.

"How are we going to get Casey through all those people?" Maya asked from the back seat, where she held the little girl on her lap. At camp, Casey had accepted some water and a few bites of pie, but had refused anything else and had clung fiercely to Maya, spending most of the ride to town with her face buried in Maya's shoulder. Sometime soon, Gage would have to interview her about what had happened to her parents, but that could wait.

"They'll let us through," he said. "The EMTs will meet us inside." He flipped on his lights and eased around the TV van, aware of a cameraman filming their arrival. He parked as close to the front door as he could. When he stepped out of the SUV, a cheer rose from the crowd. He opened the passenger door, and leaned in to help Maya and Casey out.

But when he reached in to take Casey, the little girl shrank back and shook her head. "No," she signed—a communication that was clear even to Gage.

"It's okay, honey." Maya spoke as she signed to the child. "Gage is our friend. He's just going to hold you for a little bit while I get out of the car."

Casey turned her head to look at him. The courage shining behind her fear gave rise to a fierce protectiveness in him. Some person or persons had destroyed her world with a couple of bullets, but Gage would do everything in his power to see that she wasn't hurt again.

Maya had said her niece was learning to read lips, so he looked directly at her and tried to enunciate carefully. "Will you let me hold you for just a bit while your Aunt Maya gets out of the car?" he asked. "Or you could stand here beside me?"

Casey's gaze shifted to the people who were crowding around the SUV, including the cameraman who had moved in close. "Back off and give her some room," Gage growled.

The cameraman and the others moved back, and

Gage returned his attention to Casey. "Go to Gage," Maya urged. "I'll be right here."

Casey nodded, took her arms from around Maya's neck and reached out to Gage. He picked her up and held her with as much tenderness as he could muster, as if she was made of spun sugar.

Maya climbed out of the cruiser and the reporter stepped forward, but Gage blocked him. "How did you find her?" the reporter asked.

"She came to her aunt," Gage said, as Maya took Casey once more. He put an arm around her and escorted her into the station, ignoring the reporter's follow-up questions. There would be time enough later to share the story with the rest of the world. Now, he had to take care of the child and her aunt.

Inside the station, most of the force and Adelaide waited to greet them. "We're all really happy to see you, Casey," Travis said, speaking carefully to the little girl. "How are you feeling?"

In answer, Casey buried her head in Maya's shoulder once more. "I think she's a little overwhelmed," Maya said.

"And who wouldn't be?" Adelaide stepped forward. "Let's get you both into the conference room, where it's quieter. The EMTs can check her out there. Do you think she'd like something to eat? I can make her a peanut butter sandwich with the crusts cut off. My grandchildren always liked that."

"That would be great," Maya said. She let Adelaide usher her toward the conference room, trailed by two EMTs. Gage started to follow, but Travis put a hand on his shoulder. "Tell me what happened," he said. "Then you'll need to make a statement for the press."

"We were sitting by the fire at the camp and she came out of the woods toward us, crying for Maya," Gage said. No point mentioning that seconds before, he and Maya had been kissing like reunited lovers. Even the memory of that kiss scorched him, the heat so intense and unexpected. All that talk on the drive from town about his plan to avoid getting too deeply involved with anyone, and one kiss from her had pulled him under like a riptide.

"Did she say anything about what happened to her parents?"

Travis's question pulled Gage away from his memory of that moment by the fire, back to the present. "No. She hasn't said much of anything at all," he answered.

"We need to find out what she knows," Travis said.

Gage looked toward the conference room. The door was open and he could see Casey sitting in one of the chairs, half a sandwich in one hand, a child-sized blood pressure cuff around her other arm. Maya sat to one side, her profile to the door. "Should we have a counselor or someone with us when we question her?" he asked. "If she did see her parents get shot, I don't want to traumatize her more."

Travis nodded. "Good idea. I'll contact the victim advocate program in the morning and ask them to send someone over. I'm sure they have advocates who specialize in working with children." He glanced toward the conference room. "We won't push for anything until then, but if Casey volunteers any information, we'll make note of it."

"If she wants to talk, we'll listen," Gage agreed.

The brothers went into the conference room and found the EMTs packing up their gear. "How is she?" Gage asked.

"A few bug bites and some bruises," the female EMT, Merrily Anderson, said. "She told us she drank creek water, which kept her hydrated, but it also means she was probably exposed to giardia. If any symptoms show up, she'll need to see her pediatrician. Other than that, as soon as she has a good night's sleep and a couple of good meals in her, she should be fine."

Casey laid aside the half-eaten sandwich and signed something.

"She says she lost her socks," Maya translated. She signed to the girl, speaking for the benefit of the others in the room. "We found them. We wondered why they weren't on your feet."

The girl's fingers moved rapidly in answer. "She says they got muddy, so she took them off to wash in the creek," Maya said. "She hung them on a bush to dry. Then she forgot which bush."

"Did she stay near the camp the whole time?" Gage asked. "Did she see the people looking for her?"

Maya passed on the questions and waited for the girl's answer. "She says she was afraid to go with them. And then she walked away and didn't see them anymore. When she came back, she saw me and you sitting by the fire."

"I'm so glad you saw me," Maya said as she signed, tears sliding down her cheeks. "So glad."

"Has she mentioned anything about what happened to her parents?" Travis asked.

"No." Maya gave the girl a look filled with worry. Casey had gone back to eating her sandwich. "Do you want me to ask her? I'm afraid it will upset her."

"You don't have to ask her now," Travis said. "But we'll need to know what she knows to help us find the killers."

"I know," Maya said. "I just hate to put her through that. She's been through so much already."

"We're going to bring in a victim advocate who specializes in working with children," Gage said. "She'll help us get the information we need with as little trauma as possible."

"That would definitely help." Maya stifled a yawn. "Right now, I think we're all exhausted."

"Let me take you back to the Bear's Den," Gage said. "You and Casey can both get a good night's sleep."

She glanced toward the door. "I really don't want to face that crowd again."

"I'll talk to them." Travis dug his keys from his pocket. "My Toyota is parked out back," he said, handing the keys to Gage. "Go out that way."

No one had thought to stake out the back entrance to the station, so Gage, Maya and Casey were able to leave quickly and quietly. By the time they reached the B and B, Casey had fallen asleep. She didn't wake when Gage took her in his arms. He carried her up the walkway and Paige opened the door for them.

"You must all be worn out," Paige said. "Take her straight back to Maya's room and we'll talk in the morning."

In the room, Maya folded back the covers on the big four-poster bed and Gage settled the little girl with her head on the pillow. Casey sighed as Maya pulled the covers around her and turned onto her side.

Maya looked down on her for a moment, then turned toward Gage and rested her head on his shoulder. "I'm so exhausted and relieved and grateful and sad," she said. "Thank you—for everything."

"I haven't really done anything," he said, but he tightened his arms around her and she made no protests when he pulled her close.

"You were there," she said. "I knew I could count on you. That helped. You've made me feel less alone." She rested the palm of her hand on his chest, over his heart. "When I kissed you earlier, I wasn't really planning on that. It caught me off guard." Her eyes met his and he felt a fresh jolt of heat. "But I'm not sorry it happened."

"No," he said. "I'm not sorry, either."

"Everything about the past two days is a little unreal," she said. "Including you."

She was offering him an easy out—a safe way to dismiss what had passed between them and make it about the heat of the moment. But for once, he didn't want that. He kissed her—just a brief brush of his lips across hers, then he stepped back. "Oh, I'm real all right." He took another step back. "I'll see you in the morning." He had no idea where these feelings between them were headed, but he was willing to stick around to find out.

THOUGH MAYA WAS EXHAUSTED, she lay awake a long time, Casey's little body curled next to her in the bed. Intense relief that her niece had been found safe warred with worry about their future. What did she know about raising a child—especially one who had been through such a traumatic experience? Casey was counting on her and the responsibility weighed heavily.

She finally drifted to sleep and woke with a start to find Casey watching her. "Where are we?" Casey signed.

"We're in Eagle Mountain," Maya answered. "In a house owned by a nice woman named Paige. Would you like to take a bubble bath?" The little girl was filthy, but Maya hadn't had the heart to wake her the night before to make her take a bath.

Casey nodded and sat up and swung her legs over the side of the bed, still dressed in the clothes she had worn for days. "You can wear one of my T-shirts until we get your clothes," Maya told her. She would have to ask Gage what had been done with them.

Ordinarily, a bubble bath was sure to coax a grin from the little girl, but though Casey seemed to enjoy the pampering and even played with the bubbles, mounding them in her hands and forming them into fanciful shapes, she remained solemn, her normally constantly dancing hands mostly still.

Maya had just helped her from the tub when a knock sounded on the bedroom door. Paige stood on the other side, a plastic bag in her hand. "An officer dropped these off earlier this morning," she said. "Adelaide realized Casey would need clean clothes, so she talked the sheriff into releasing them."

"Bless her." Maya took the bag. "And thank you."

Paige glanced toward the open bathroom door. "I heard the water running and thought it was probably safe to come up. I wanted to let you sleep as long as possible. I know you're both exhausted."

"Once I finally got to sleep, I pretty much passed out," Maya said.

Paige lowered her voice. "How is she?"

"Quiet. Quieter than usual. And serious. More serious than a five-year-old should be."

Paige reached out and squeezed Maya's shoulder. "I imagine it will take time. But being with you is going to help her. Clearly, she trusts you."

Casey trusted Maya to do the right thing, but Maya had no clue what that might be. She felt a tug on her shirt and looked down to find Casey, wrapped in the oversized bath towel. "Paige brought your clothes." Maya spoke and signed, then held up the plastic bag.

Casey took the bag and stood staring at Paige.

Paige squatted down so that she was at Casey's level. "Do you like waffles?" she asked.

Casey looked up at Maya and Maya translated the words into American Sign Language. "She's still learning lipreading," she told Paige. "And yes, she loves waffles."

"Then as soon as you're dressed and come downstairs, I'll make you one—with whipped cream and strawberries, if you like."

Casey nodded and trotted back to the bathroom with the bag containing her clothes. When the door had closed behind her, Maya turned back to Paige. "Gage said the sheriff's office will have a victim advocate who specializes in children present when they question her."

"And you'll be there, too, I imagine," Paige said. "Are you her guardian now?"

She didn't say *now that your sister is dead*—Maya appreciated that. "Yes. When Angela and Greg talked to me about it when they made their will, I never expected it was something I would really have to do. It's such a big responsibility and I haven't a clue."

"You love her and that will go a long way toward leading you in the right direction, I believe," Paige said. "And there are a lot of people you can ask for help."

"When we get back to Denver, I want to find a counselor for Casey to see—someone who can help her deal with everything she's been through."

"That's a great idea. Has she said anything about her parents?"

"No. And I can't decide if that's bad or not."

"I think it's probably normal." Paige stepped back. "Come down when you're ready. I'll have fresh coffee and those waffles."

Casey emerged from the bathroom a few moments later, dressed in a denim skirt and a pink tee, a hairbrush in her hand. "I need help with my hair," she signed.

"Come sit on the bed and I'll fix it for you."

Calm settled over Maya as she went through the familiar, soothing motions of brushing her niece's hair and fastening it into a ponytail. The two had spent many happy afternoons playing hairdresser, taking turns combing and styling each other's hair, laughing at some of the crazy results they had achieved.

At last, she laid aside the brush. "How about some breakfast?" she asked Casey.

The little girl nodded.

Downstairs, Maya was relieved to see that they would be alone with Paige. "Where are your other guests?" she asked as Paige set a mug of steaming coffee in front of her.

"I just have two other couples here right now. They left early this morning to go climbing." She set plates in front of them filled with golden waffles drizzled with strawberry syrup, more berries and mounds of whipped cream on top. Casey's eyes widened, and her expression held more life than Maya had seen since she and her niece had been reunited.

"I think she approves," she said, and picked up her own fork.

They were just finishing the waffles when the doorbell rang. A few seconds later, Paige returned to the room, followed by Gage—a Gage who wore a starched uniform and smelled of a woodsy aftershave. Maya's heart thudded wildly as he filled the doorway to the dining room, and she struggled to maintain her composure. Memory of the incendiary kiss they had shared by the campfire rushed back.

A tug on her shirt allowed her to tear her gaze away from him and focus on her niece. "Why are your cheeks so red?" the little girl signed.

The question only made Maya blush more. "I must have eaten too fast," she answered—a completely ridiculous reply, but all she could think of at the moment. "You remember Gage, don't you?" she added.

Casey nodded. She began signing, fingers moving rapidly.

"What's she saying?" Gage asked.

"She says she saw you with me. By that little building. And the man was shooting at you." Maya's voice caught. "She says she ran away because she was afraid the man would hurt us, the way he hurt her mommy and daddy." As Maya finished speaking, Casey put her face in her hands and began to sob.

Maya slid out of her chair and gathered Casey to her. "It's all right, honey," she murmured, rocking the child against her and smoothing her hair. "I'm not hurt. I'm okay." Even though she knew Casey couldn't hear her, she needed to say the words.

Gage squatted down beside the chair. "Ask her if the man who was shooting at you and me was the same one who hurt her parents," he said.

"I can't do that," Maya said. "Can't you see how upset she is? We need to wait for the victim advocate."

Gage's jaw tightened, and she could almost hear his teeth grinding together, but he stood. "She's supposed to be here at ten, so I thought I could give you a ride to the station."

"I can drive over in my car," Maya said.

"You could. But it will be easier to get through the reporters if you're with me."

"Reporters?" Maya glanced over at Paige.

"I hadn't mentioned them yet," Paige said. "They've been gathered outside since dawn. And the crowd is growing. I had three calls this morning from national networks. I finally had to take the phone off the hook." She frowned at Gage. "Can't you do something about them? They're interfering with my business."

"As long as they're not trespassing on your property, there's not a lot we can do," Gage said. He returned his attention to Maya. "Travis thinks we should have a press conference this morning, and let them take some pictures. It's up to you whether you want to grant any other interviews, or allow Casey to speak to them."

"Absolutely not." She stood, one hand still on Casey's shoulder. "I'll do the press conference, but I won't allow them to talk to Casey. Fortunately, she won't be able to hear their questions."

"Let's schedule the conference for one. That will give us time to meet with the victim advocate first." He stepped back. "We'll leave when you're finished with your breakfast."

Maya looked down at Casey's mostly empty plate. "I think we're done." She put her hand on the girl's cheek, capturing her attention. "Let's go wash your face and you can brush your teeth, then we're going to go with Deputy Walker for a while," she signed and spoke.

Casey sniffed and scrubbed at her eyes, then climbed out of her chair and carefully pushed it back into the table. "I'll wait by the door," Gage said.

Maya nodded, breakfast sitting like a rock in her stomach. She knew Gage needed the information Casey could give them in order to find Angela and Greg's murderers, but seeing the little girl upset tore her apart. She trusted Gage, but she didn't think she could keep quiet if he did anything to hurt her niece.

Chapter Eleven

The three of them braved the gauntlet of reporters, Casey hiding her face against Maya's shoulder and Gage walking with his arm around them both. He ignored the shouted questions and kept his focus forward. He realized they had jobs to do, but behind the feel-good story of a lost child who had been found lay a double murder and a lot of pain. He saw no need to put that suffering on display for the public.

Nobody said much of anything on the ride to the station. Though Gage hadn't spent a lot of time around children, Casey struck him as too quiet for a five-year-old. She sat in the booster seat he'd borrowed from the department and stared listlessly out the window. Maya was quiet, too. He could feel tension radiating off her—and more than a little resentment at him, that he had brought the little girl to tears. Couldn't she see he had a job to do? A job that required him to do ugly and yes, sometimes hurtful, things? He didn't want to hurt a little girl, but the longer they waited to find out the information she could give him, the more time a killer or killers had to get away—and maybe even to kill again.

When the three of them entered the sheriff's office—through the back door again—a silver-haired woman in a dark purple suit stepped forward to meet them. "I'm Darla Rivers," she said, offering her hand. "I'm the victim advocate." She shook hands with Maya, then smiled down at Casey. "Hello, Casey," she signed as she spoke. "My name is Darla, and I hope we're going to be friends."

"You know ASL," Maya said.

"Yes. Casey isn't the first deaf child I've worked with." She moved to the sofa in a small waiting area and sat down. "Casey, would you and your aunt come sit with me?" she asked.

Maya led Casey to the sofa, where the little girl settled between the two women. Talking and signing, Darla explained that her job as a victim advocate was to be Casey's friend and to look after her interests and what was best for her—no matter what anyone else in the room thought. Casey listened intently, but Gage wondered how much a child that young could understand.

"Deputy Walker and the sheriff need to ask you some questions about what happened in the woods," Darla continued, signing as she spoke. "I know it might be hard to answer some of their questions, but anything you can remember will help them to catch the bad people who did this. Are you ready to try to help us?"

Casey hesitated, then took Maya's hand and nodded. Gage glanced at Travis.

Travis sat and pulled his chair closer to the sofa. Gage did the same. "We're videotaping this interview," Travis explained. "That allows us to capture all the sign language—Casey's language—and we also may be able to use the tape as evidence in court, so that Casey doesn't have to testify in person."

"That's good," Maya said.

Travis turned to Casey. The little girl stared back at him. She didn't look intimidated, but determined. In fact, her expression mirrored that of her aunt. Maya gripped the child with one hand and kept the other hand in a fist resting on her thigh.

Darla opened a large satchel and took out a drawing pad and some colored markers. She handed these to Casey. "I thought we would start by having you draw us a picture," she explained. "Draw a picture of what happened in the woods, when the bad people came."

Casey looked doubtful, and turned a purple marker over and over in her hand. "Go ahead," Maya urged. "You're very good at drawing."

After a moment, Casey put aside the purple marker and chose a black one. She began to make marks on the paper—a tent. Trees. The campfire. She put a little stick figure in the tent, lying down. That would be Casey, Gage guessed. Then two stick figures by the fire, one with long hair—her mother and father? The marker hovered over the page, then Casey bent low, shielding her work with her body, the marker squeaking against the pad. A tear fell on the page, making the marker run, and then another. Casey dropped the marker and turned her head away.

Darla handed the child a tissue and rubbed her shoulder, then slipped the pad from her lap. She studied the drawing a moment, then handed it to Travis. Gage leaned over to look at the drawing. Casey had added two figures in black—larger than the others. One of the figures held what was clearly a gun, and the little girl had drawn dashed lines from the gun to both her parents. The starkness of the scene made Gage feel a little sick—and angry that a child had had to witness such a thing.

"This is good," Travis said, addressing Casey, even though she wasn't looking at him. He turned to Darla. "Ask her if she can describe the shooters—were they male or female, tall, short, fat, thin? Did they have beards or wear glasses? Did they say anything? Did they argue with her parents and if so, what about? Did she see what kind of vehicle they were in?"

Darla nodded and began signing. Casey stared, wide-eyed, then began shaking her head back and forth, hair flying. Then she whimpered and turned away, and crawled into Maya's lap, her sobbing the only sound.

Maya wrapped her arms around the child. "We have to stop," she said. "This is too upsetting."

Travis looked grim. "We need more information if we're going to catch these two."

"Let's take a break and calm down," Darla said. "Then we can try again." She touched Maya's shoulder. "Let me take her for a little bit. You go outside and get some fresh air."

She nodded and left. Gage stared after her. "Maybe I should go talk to her," he said.

"It's your funeral," Travis said.

Outside, Gage found Maya leaning against the brick of the building, arms folded across her chest. She glanced at him when he came to stand beside her, but quickly looked away. "If you came out here to try to talk me into letting you bully Casey with your questions, you're wasting your breath," she said.

"I'm not bullying her and you know it." He leaned against the brick also, so close their shoulders were almost touching. "Did you ever think that it might be good for her to talk about what happened? That talking might make it less scary for her?"

"So you're a child psychologist now?" She turned on him. "A couple of nutcases destroyed her world and you want her to keep reliving that moment?"

"I want to find those two nutcases and stop them." He took hold of her arm, as much because he wanted that physical contact as to stop her from storming away from him. "Did it occur to you that if the people who did this find out Casey saw them, they could come after her? We need to find them before they do that."

All the color left her face and if not for his hand steadying her, he thought she might have fallen. "Come after her?" she whispered. "Gage, no—you can't let that happen."

"I don't intend to. But I need to know what she knows. Every little thing she can tell us is more than we have to go on right now. I don't want to hurt her, but more than that, I don't want them to hurt her."

She nodded and pulled away. He let her go. "If Darla thinks it's okay, you can question Casey some more," she said. "I'll try not to let my own anxieties influence her."

"I know it's not easy for you," he said. "But think of it this way—Casey survived two nights in the woods on her own. She's a very tough little girl. A very brave one."

"She is, isn't she?" She no longer looked so pale, and some of the bleakness had receded from her eyes. "Thanks for reminding me of that."

"Let's give her a little more time to recover," he said. "In the meantime, I need you to do something."

"Oh?" She eyed him warily.

"I need you to look at Angela and Greg's belongings and see if there's anything out of place," he said. "It can be disturbing, seeing things that belonged to someone you loved, laid out this way, tagged as evidence in a crime. But I need you to try to put aside the emotion and be as objective as possible. We can study these items all day and not see what you can see in a few minutes. We need to know if anything strikes you as out of place or not right or not characteristic of your sister and her husband."

"All right," Maya said. "If you think it will help."

"I don't know if it will help, but I'm determined to do everything I can to find their killers. They deserve that much." He put his hand on her shoulder and looked

her in the eye, hoping she would see the emotion behind his words. "You and Casey deserve that, too."

GAGE'S WORDS—AND the look in his eyes—touched
Maya. But the thought of doing what he asked, looking through objects that had been so close to Angela
and Greg, hurt. She took a deep breath, fighting for a
calm she didn't feel. This was important. She couldn't
bring Angela back to life, but she could do this one
thing to help Gage and his fellow officers find Angela
and Greg's killers. "I'm ready," she said.

He led her back inside and into a standard conference room of beige walls and gray tile floor. Banks
of fluorescent lighting cast a harsh white light over
the items laid out on long tables in the center of the
room. Maya scanned the collection and recognized a
blue-and-white cooler that had held drinks at countless
backyard barbecues and two blue plastic storage containers of the kind her sister used for storing everything
from Christmas decorations to out-of-season clothing.
Next to the storage containers, someone had arranged
what she assumed was the contents of the containers—
canned food, paper plates and plastic utensils, a blue
tarp, first aid kit and rain gear. A camping stove, lantern, two camp chairs, a backpack, some books and
Angela's purse completed the collection of evidence.

Seeing the purse here hurt the most. The bag was
light blue leather, with a silver butterfly charm dangling from the strap. Maya had been with Angela when
she purchased the bag, both women crowing over the
fact that it had been marked down 40 percent off at

"One Minute" Survey

You get **TWO books** <u>and</u> TWO Mystery Gifts...

ABSOLUTELY FREE!

YOU pick your books – WE pay for everything!

See inside for details.

YOU pick your books –
WE pay for everything.
You get TWO new books and TWO Mystery Gifts...
absolutely FREE!
Total retail value: Over $20!

Dear Reader,

Your opinions are important to us. So if you'll participate in our fast and free "One Minute" Survey, **YOU** can pick two wonderful books that **WE** pay for!

As a leading publisher of women's fiction, we'd love to hear from you. That's why we promise to reward you for completing our survey.

IMPORTANT: Please complete the survey and return it. We'll send your Free Books and Free Mystery Gifts right away. **And we pay for shipping and handling too!**

Thank you again for participating in our ↖ *We pay*
"One Minute" Survey. It really takes just a minute *EVERYT*
(or less) to complete the survey... and your free books and gifts will be well worth it!

Sincerely,

Pam Powers

Pam Powers
for Reader Service

"One Minute" Survey

GET YOUR FREE BOOKS AND FREE GIFTS!

✓ Complete this Survey   ✓ Return this survey

◄ DETACH AND MAIL CARD TODAY! ▼

1 Do you try to find time to read every day?
☐ YES   ☐ NO

2 Do you prefer books which reflect Christian values?
☐ YES   ☐ NO

3 Do you enjoy having books delivered to your home?
☐ YES   ☐ NO

4 Do you find a Larger Print size easier on your eyes?
☐ YES   ☐ NO

YES! I have completed the above "One Minute" Survey. Please send me my Two Free Books and Two Free Mystery Gifts (worth over $20 retail). I understand that I am under no obligation to buy anything, as explained on the back of this card.

❏ I prefer the regular-print edition
182/382 HDL GM3V

❏ I prefer the larger-print edition
199/399 HDL GM3V

FIRST NAME	LAST NAME

ADDRESS

APT.#	CITY

STATE/PROV.	ZIP/POSTAL CODE

© 2017 HARLEQUIN ENTERPRISES LIMITED
® and ™ are trademarks owned and used by the trademark owner and/or its licensee. Printed in the U.S.A.

▲ If offer card is missing write to: Reader Service, P.O. Box 1341, Buffalo, NY 14240-8531 or visit www.ReaderService.com ▲

BUSINESS REPLY MAIL

FIRST-CLASS MAIL   PERMIT NO. 717   BUFFALO, NY

POSTAGE WILL BE PAID BY ADDRESSEE

READER SERVICE
PO BOX 1341
BUFFALO NY 14240-8571

NO POSTAGE
NECESSARY
IF MAILED
IN THE
UNITED STATES

an end-of-season clearance sale. She approached the bag warily, cringing at the bright yellow Evidence tag attached next to the butterfly charm. "You can touch anything you want," Gage said. He waited by the door, as if giving her room to process all of this.

She picked up the wallet—a red leather one their mother had sent for Christmas last year. Maya had one just like it. "Angela used to say she kept her whole life in her purse," she said. She opened her wallet to reveal a driver's license and half a dozen loyalty cards for grocery stores and a pharmacy, a single credit card and a library card. The money compartment held nine dollar bills and the change compartment was empty. "She never kept much cash. She preferred to use her credit card for everything."

She set aside the wallet and considered the assortment of tissues, lipsticks, bandages, pens, makeup and a cell phone that made up the rest of the contents of the purse. She picked up the phone and debated turning it on. "We checked out the phone," Gage said. "No calls after the one she made to you the day they arrived in Eagle Mountain."

"She wanted to let me know she got here all right." Her voice broke and she set the phone back on the table, fighting for composure. She couldn't break down now—not yet. She had to keep it together, for Angela and Greg. Gage remained by the door, though she sensed him poised to spring into action, perhaps even to pull her out of the room if she started to go over the edge.

The idea strengthened her and she moved on to the

backpack and its contents. Here was her brother-in-law, Greg—the always-prepared scientist, with his first aid kit, ordinance maps, binoculars, granola bars and books. She picked up the top volume on the small stack of reading material. *"A History of Mines and Mining in Rayford County,"* she read aloud. "That sounds like Greg."

She set the book aside and stared at the rest of the items laid out on the table. Grief dragged at her, like one of those lead aprons the dental assistant draped over her before she took X-rays. She shook her head. "I don't see anything unusual or out of place," she said. "They were just two ordinary people. There was no reason for this to happen." The last word came out in a sob she was unable to hold back. She bowed her head, then felt strong arms come around her. She turned into Gage and rested her head against the hard wall of his chest and sobbed, giving in to the grief and the opportunity to let someone else hold her up for a few moments.

By the time her tears were spent, his shirt was soaked and she was embarrassed, but still she kept her eyes closed and didn't move. Here in his arms was so safe and warm, and as she rested there, she became aware of other sensations—his clean, masculine smell and the steady, strong rhythm of his heartbeat, the solid bulge of muscles in his arms, and the way her own body warmed to his appealing masculinity. Here was a reminder, in the midst of the worst time of her life, that she was still very much alive and grateful for all that entailed.

Gage eased her away from him, though he kept his hands on her upper arms. "Better?" he asked.

She nodded. "But your shirt…"

"I have another one in my locker." He glanced toward the items on the table. "Thanks for taking a look. I know it was difficult."

"I wish I had seen something that could help you. I feel so helpless."

"You can't see what isn't there. And you are helping. You're a living, breathing reminder of what we're working for. Not that we wouldn't give our best, regardless. But sometimes, seeing how what we do impacts real lives is the incentive we need to put in another hour or dig a little deeper. We won't give up."

Watching him as he spoke, the intensity in his eyes and the emotion behind his words, she believed him. She trusted him. She had known Gage Walker less than two days, yet already she believed she could trust him with her life.

WHEN GAGE AND Maya rejoined Casey and Darla, they found the two coloring. They were working on a drawing that depicted all kinds of flowers—a much happier drawing than the all-black picture Casey had drawn for them. Gage took his seat across from them once more, and Maya perched on the end of the sofa. Travis joined them. "Did you see any flowers while you were in the woods?" Travis asked.

They waited while Darla conveyed his question in sign language. As the conversation continued, she served as translator.

Casey focused on filling in the petals of a large daisy with a pink marker, setting aside the color to sign. "I saw some yellow ones and purple ones," she signed. She replaced the cap on the pink marker and chose a yellow one. "I ate some raspberries. They were really good."

"That was smart of you, to find and eat the raspberries," Gage said.

She shrugged. "I was hungry."

"You said you saw me and your Aunt Maya by the little building," Gage said. "What were you doing when you saw us?"

"I saw the buildings and thought there might be food there, or someplace warm to sleep. But all the doors I tried were locked, but then I saw you and Aunt Maya."

"What happened then?" Travis asked.

"I was going to go to you, but then I saw the men talking. So I hid and watched. Then I saw it was one of the men—one of the bad men." She pressed her lips tightly together.

"So you ran away," Gage said, very gently.

She nodded and made a sign that Gage could clearly understand as going away—one finger drawn from one side to the other across her body. Then she began to sign more rapidly, and he was grateful for Darla's translation.

"I saw them shooting, and I was so afraid they had hurt Aunt Maya. I ran and ran until I couldn't run anymore. And then I didn't know where I was."

"You said one man," Travis said. "There was only one man who shot at your aunt and Deputy Walker?"

Casey nodded.

"And there were two men who shot your mom and dad?" Travis asked. "And the man who shot at your aunt and Deputy Walker was one of them?"

Another nod.

"Was he a big man?" Travis asked. "Was he bigger than Deputy Walker?"

She studied Gage, sizing him up, then made a sign that clearly conveyed the man she'd seen was shorter, but broader, a fact Darla confirmed.

"What color was his hair?" Travis asked.

Casey shook her head and continued to sign.

"She says he was wearing a hat," Darla said. "A knit cap, I think. It was black. All his clothes were black."

"What about the second man?" Travis asked. "The one who was with this one at camp?"

Casey took a deep breath, the struggle to remember—or maybe all the sadness that went with remembering—playing out across her face. Then she began a series of rapid signs—too rapid for Gage to follow. "The other man was about as tall as Deputy Walker," Darla said. "But…thicker. I think she means bulkier. He had a gun, too. She doesn't know which one shot her mother and father. Maybe both of them."

Casey leaned against Maya and closed her eyes. "I think she's had enough questions for today," Darla said.

"Just one more question," Travis said. "Is there anything else she wants us to know?"

Darla tapped Casey's arm to get her attention, then relayed the question. Casey looked at Gage, eyes big and bright with unshed tears. She made a series of signs he tried hard to understand, but could not. Darla gasped.

"What is it?" Gage asked. "What did she say?"

"She says the tall, bulky man saw her peeking out of the tent. He looked right at her and she thinks he shouted," Darla said. "He may have tried to follow her but she got away. But she's very afraid he will try to come after her and hurt her, too."

Chapter Twelve

Darla's words sent a cold shard of fear through Maya. Her first instinct was to grab Casey and pull her close, but she didn't want to alarm the little girl. Casey was counting on the adults around her to keep her safe, so Maya couldn't let her niece see her fear. She put a hand on Casey's head. The little girl looked at her, her eyes intent. "I'll protect you," Maya signed, though she had no idea how to do that.

"We should go back to Denver," she said out loud. "We'll be safer there."

Gage took her arm. "Darla, you and Travis stay with Casey while Maya and I talk."

Maya started to protest that she didn't want to leave Casey right now, but the look in Gage's eyes warned her he wasn't going to take no for an answer. Arguing in front of the child didn't seem like the best choice, so she reluctantly followed Gage into his office.

He shut the door and faced her. "Running away to Denver is a bad idea," he said.

"I'm not running away," she said. "Denver is my home. It's Casey's home."

"I don't think it's safe," he said. "The killers could follow you there."

"It will be harder to find us in a big city."

"How hard will it be for them to find out where you work—where you live?" he asked. "Once they know that, they can watch you and learn where Casey goes to school." He moved closer, until his chest was almost touching hers. The move could have been threatening, but it only reminded her of how close they had been around that campfire. The memory flashed across her mind at the feel of his arms around her, his body pressed against hers. She pushed it away. She didn't want to remember that moment—she couldn't remember it right now.

"Eagle Mountain is a small town," he continued. "Strangers and suspicious people stand out. You'll have the whole town watching out for you here."

Everything he said made sense, but it didn't lessen her urge to run and hide. "I need time to think," she said.

"I don't want you to go," he said.

She stared at him, her heart racing painfully. "I'm not sure what you mean."

"Yes, you do." He moved closer still, their bodies touching now. "You knew it when you kissed me there by the campfire. I never intended for it to happen, but I care about you. And I care about Casey. I want to help you protect her. I want to protect both of you."

She tried to swallow, her mouth dry as she remembered the ferocity of that kiss, how that moment with him had cut through all the fear and uncertainty. And she remembered afterward, too, when he had been so gentle with Casey. The little girl had trusted him, at a time when she had every reason not to trust a stranger. She spread her palms on his chest, not pushing him away, but giving herself a little space. "This isn't a good time for this," she said. "For us."

"You're right—it isn't. And it would be an easy out for me to use bad timing as an excuse to step back from this, but I won't. I can't."

"I need time to think," she said again.

He must have heard the desperation behind the words. He stepped back. "Think all you want," he said. "But do it here, where I can help you and Casey."

"I'd better go to her," she said. "She'll be wondering where I am."

Casey was so engrossed in conversation with Darla that she scarcely looked up when Maya and Gage returned. "I was telling her about my cats," Darla said. "One of them is a real goofball."

"Thanks for distracting her," Maya said. "And thank you for all your help today."

"That's my job, but it's also something I enjoy a great deal." Darla pressed a business card into Maya's hand. "I'm officially Casey's advocate now, so call me if you need anything at all. And I'll be checking in with you again soon."

"Let's go back to the B and B and see about lunch," Maya signed to Casey.

They said goodbye to Darla, and started across the lobby with Gage when Adelaide called to them. "Come over here a minute," she said. "There's something I want to show you."

The three of them moved to Adelaide's desk. "All of this is for you," she said, pulling out a plastic box filled with cards and several stuffed animals. "People have been dropping them off since yesterday."

Maya translated this news to Casey, whose eyes widened. The little girl plucked a pink rabbit from the box and squeezed it to her chest. Maya blinked back sudden tears. "I don't know what to say," she said.

"The whole town is so glad to know that Casey is safe." Adelaide handed her one of the cards. "You should read a few."

Maya slid the card from the envelope and opened it. *I helped with the search and stayed up nights worrying about that little girl. I cried tears of joy when I heard the news she was safe. I'm so sorry you both have had to go through such sorrow, but remember you are really a part of all of us now. Best wishes for a happy future. Barbara.*

Maya stared at the mound of cards in the box. "This is amazing."

"You take them home and read through them." Adelaide handed over the box. "We opened them all, just to make sure there were no nasty-grams. I'm sorry it has to be that way, but you can't be too careful."

"I understand," she said.

While Maya and Casey looked through more of the cards, Maya was dimly aware of the front door to the station opening. She glanced back at the stocky man in a red T-shirt who entered. "Hey, Gage, you're just the man I wanted to see," the newcomer said. "I might have a lead on those thefts from the high school."

"Would you mind waiting just a minute?" Gage asked her.

"Go ahead. We'll be fine waiting here." Casey hadn't even looked up from the cards. A stuffed animal under each arm, she traced one finger over a colorful photograph of wildflowers on the front of one card. Later, when they were alone, Maya would ask her niece what she thought of this outpouring of support. For Maya, it helped ease her pain a little to know they weren't alone.

GAGE LED WADE Tomlinson into his office and shut the door behind them. "What can I do for you?" Gage asked.

"Is that little Casey out there?" Wade asked. "She looks like she's doing pretty good for a kid who was lost in the woods for two nights."

"She's a remarkable little girl." And her aunt was a remarkable woman—one who had turned Gage's easygoing life upside down. "What did you want to talk to me about?"

Wade lowered his stocky frame into the chair across from Gage's desk. "You said you wanted to know anything that might help you track down the school robbers. I might have something, though I don't know if it will really be any help to you."

The high school case seemed to have happened weeks ago, though Gage realized it had only been two days since the second break-in. He sat behind his desk and picked up a pen, prepared to make notes. "What have you got?"

"Brock and I were climbing over in Shakes Canyon yesterday afternoon and we ran into two guys we haven't seen around here before. Young skinhead types—you know the kind—shaved heads and Nazi tattoos. Bad attitudes. I talked to them a little—they said they're camped out in the woods south of town. I'm not saying they're the ones behind the vandalism, but something about them struck me as wrong, you know?"

It wasn't much to go on, but it wouldn't hurt to give these two a closer look. "Thanks," Gage said. "We'll check them out."

Wade stood. "Something about them wasn't right," he said. "And I don't mean just the Nazi stuff. Maybe they had something to do with the shooting of that little girl's parents."

"We aren't ruling out anyone at this point." He stood also, and moved toward the door.

"Has Casey been able to give you a description of the killer or anything?" Wade asked.

"She's told us some. We're still working with her on that."

"Yeah. I guess little kids aren't the most reliable witnesses."

"Casey is reliable," Gage said. "She's going to be a big help to us."

He escorted Wade out, then joined Maya and Casey

at Adelaide's desk. "Look at all this," Maya said, indicating the bin full of cards and toys. "I still can't believe people brought them for Casey. It's amazing."

"Everybody was concerned about her," he said. "We're all glad she's safe." He squeezed her shoulder, hoping she would understand that he would do everything in his power to keep her that way.

He picked up the bin and she and Casey followed him out to his cruiser. "Did that man know who took those items from the high school?" Maya asked, as she fastened Casey into the booster seat in the back of the SUV.

"He had an idea about a couple of people he thought I should check out—I'll follow up on them."

Casey, still clutching the pink bunny, tugged on Maya's sleeve. When she had her aunt's attention, she signed. Maya smiled. "She says she's going to name the bunny Bitty Bunny."

"Cute name," Gage said.

When they were all buckled in, Gage started the cruiser and headed out onto Eagle Mountain's main street. "Is sign language hard to learn?" he asked.

"American Sign Language isn't any more difficult than any other language," Maya said. "Easier than most, I imagine. We all started learning it as soon as Casey was born and it didn't seem like it took that long. I guess the main difference is that it's a physical language instead of a spoken one. The movements of your fingers and hands are important, but so is your expression."

"I've been watching you and Casey talk," he said. "It's like you're communicating with your whole bodies."

"In a way, we are. I think it's a very beautiful language."

"I'd like to learn," he said. "It would probably help me in my work."

Maya turned to face Casey. *"I'm telling her you want to learn sign language,"* she said. "She says you should—then the two of you could talk."

He pulled the cruiser to the curb in front of the Bear's Den. "I'll stop by when I get off shift this evening," he said.

"You don't—" She stopped and shook her head. "That would be great," she said, and turned to help Casey.

He watched them make their way up the walk and into the B and B. She had been about to tell him that he didn't need to stop by—that they would be fine without him. He wondered what had changed her mind. Was she beginning to see him as an important part of her life?

He pulled away from the curb, thoughts churning. Maybe he should let Maya do what she wanted and take Casey back to Denver. He could talk to the police there and arrange for them to keep an eye on her. That would be the easiest solution. Without them here, he would be freer to focus on his work and go back to the no-hassles, stress-free personal life he had worked hard to put together these last few years.

His head told him that was the right thing to do—but he wasn't so sure his heart was down with that plan.

MAYA SET THE box of cards and toys on the table in the hall. Paige had left a note, her writing a cramped scrawl on a piece of torn notebook paper. *Out running errands,* it read. *The other guests are out as well. I have a new couple checking in this afternoon. I should be home before they arrive, but if they show up early, their check-in packet is on my desk in my office, next to the dining room.*

"I'm hungry," Casey signed.

"I'll see if there's anything in the kitchen for lunch." Maya set the note aside. "You take the stuffed animals upstairs to our room. We can look through the cards together after we eat."

Casey grabbed a blue bear and a purple hippo out of the bin and raced up the stairs with them and the pink bunny. Maya felt a little lighter as she listened to the girl's feet pound up the stairs. It was such a normal kid noise—and maybe a sign that the trauma she had endured hadn't permanently damaged her.

In the kitchen, she found tuna, mayonnaise, pickles and bread. She decided to make tuna sandwiches. Later, she would go shopping and replace the supplies, but she didn't think Paige would begrudge them to her now. She would look for something special as a gift for their hostess as well—maybe some good chocolates or fancy cookies.

She was assembling the sandwiches when she thought she heard the front door open. "Paige, I'm in here," she called.

But Paige didn't answer. Maya finished making lunch and washed her hands, but she couldn't shake the certainty that she had heard the front door. "Paige?" she called again, and moved into the front room.

No one was there, and a glance out the front window showed Paige's car wasn't parked at the curb or in the driveway. Maybe Maya had imagined the noise. Her nerves had certainly been on edge the past few days. Maybe what she had heard had just been the normal settling of a place this old. She started up the stairs to tell Casey lunch was ready.

Halfway up, a strangled scream broke the afternoon silence. "Casey!" Maya shouted, and ran up the remaining stairs. She raced toward the closed door to the bedroom she and Casey shared and was struggling with the knob when pain exploded at the back of her head and everything went black.

Chapter Thirteen

"We are still interviewing Casey about what happened to her," Travis told the assembled reporters. "We're working with specialists to make sure we get everything she can tell us about the killer or killers, without causing her any more pain than necessary. In the meantime, we are investigating other angles of this case. I'm confident we are going to track down these people and stop them."

Some of the crowd gathered in the conference room at the Rayford County Sheriff's Department applauded as Travis completed his prepared statement to the press, while other hands flew into the air and reporters began firing questions. Gage stood next to and slightly behind his brother, studying the crowd. The mayor was here, impatiently shifting from foot to foot and glowering at the crowd, as the sheriff responded to six variations of the same question, which was asked first by a reporter from the Denver paper. "Who do you think did this and why?"

"Our investigation is ongoing." Travis repeated this and variations of the phrase for the next ten minutes until Gage, on a prearranged signal, stepped forward and took the microphone. "Thank you all for coming today," he said. "That's all the questions we have time for."

Mayor Larry Rowe moved to the microphone. "I'd just like to say that the town of Eagle Mountain is shocked and horrified by these recent events," he said. "And that this is not at all in keeping with the character of our town and its citizens." He glared out at the room, as if expecting questions, but another officer was already ushering the press out of the room.

Gage waited until the mayor had also left, then turned to Travis. "Want to ride out and look for these two skinheads Wade reported?"

"Where do you plan to start looking?" Travis asked.

"They were climbing in Shakes Canyon. We'll start there."

The two brothers left the conference room. Adelaide hurried toward them. "Dispatch just requested a unit report to 192 Elm Court," she said. "They got a 911 call from that address, but no response."

It took half a second for the address to register. "That's the Bear's Den," he said. "Who made the call?"

"The dispatcher says the line is still open, but she's not getting any response."

Gage was running now, Travis right behind him, already on the line to dispatch. "Put out a call for backup," he ordered.

Gage raced to his SUV. He had dropped off Maya and Casey less than twenty minutes ago and they had been fine. He should have gone into the house with them. What if the killer had discovered where they were staying and had been in there waiting for them? Gage should have thought of that.

He pulled the cruiser to the curb and cut the engine. Travis pulled in behind him. A quick glance showed nothing untoward about the house's appearance. The front door was closed and everything on the outside looked in order. One hand on the weapon at his side, he hurried up the walk, Travis at his side.

The front door, which should have been locked, opened easily when he turned the knob. He shoved it open and waited a second before he peered carefully around the frame. No sign of a disturbance in the front hall. "Maya!" he shouted. "Paige! It's me, Gage."

No answer.

"Paige's car isn't out front," Travis said.

Struggling to control his racing heart, Gage drew his weapon and started for the stairs. Halfway up, he heard what might have been crying and ran the rest of the way, to the hallway, where he spotted Maya, slumped on the floor in front of the door to one of the bedrooms.

He dropped to his knees beside her, relief leaving him weak when he realized she was alive and breathing. Blood seeped around a lump at the back of her head, but the pulse in her neck beat steadily beneath his fingers and as he carefully rolled her over, her eyes fluttered and she groaned.

"It's okay. You're going to be okay." He gently rubbed her hand between his palms and she opened her eyes and stared up at him, gradually bringing him into focus.

"Gage," she said softly. And then louder. "Gage!" She tried to sit up, but he pushed her back.

"Take it easy," he said. "You've got a knot the size of a hen egg on the back of your head. What happened?"

"Someone hit me, I think." She fought against his hold and this time, he let her sit up. "Casey!" she said. "We have to find Casey."

Gage helped Maya to her feet. She swayed and held on to him, then steadied herself. "Did you call 911?" Travis asked.

"No. Is that why you're here?"

"Dispatch said they received a call from this address, but no one said anything."

"Casey knows to call 911 in an emergency," Maya said. "Angie and Greg taught her that." She groped for the knob on the bedroom door. "I heard a scream and was on my way in here when someone hit me."

The door opened to reveal an attractively furnished bedroom with a neatly made four-poster bed, antique dresser and slipper chair. A purple stuffed hippo lay on the floor in front of a closed door. Maya, Gage close behind her, hurried to the door. She tried to turn the knob, but it wouldn't budge. "It's locked," she said, and began pounding on the door.

"If Casey's in there, she may have locked herself in to get away from whoever hit you," Gage said. He glanced around the room and spotted an empty phone cradle. "Was there a phone in there?" he asked.

Maya frowned at the base unit, which sat on the bedside table. "I guess so. I hadn't really paid attention.

I always make calls on my cell phone." She pounded on the door. "Casey!" Her face twisted in anguish. "I know she can't hear me, but I don't know what else to do. What if she's in there and hurt?"

"Let me see." Gage gently moved her aside and examined the doorknob. "Do you have a paper clip?" he asked.

"Maybe in my purse."

"Get it. I think I can insert it in this hole here and pop the lock." He indicated the small hole at the base of the doorknob.

She moved away and returned a few moments later with a paper clip. He straightened one end and inserted it into the hole. Something clicked and he was able to turn the knob.

Maya rushed in ahead of him. She pulled back the shower curtain to reveal Casey huddled in a small ball at one end of the tub, the pink stuffed rabbit clutched in one hand, the phone in the other. Maya lifted the sobbing girl from the tub and Gage took the phone. "This is Deputy Walker," he told the dispatcher. "Everything's under control here. You can cancel that call for backup."

"Ten-four."

"I'll search the rest of the house," Travis said, and left them.

Gage ended the call and laid the phone on the bathroom vanity. Maya had set the little girl on the side of the tub and was signing to her. Casey didn't answer at first, but then her fingers began to move, with small gestures at first, then with more assurance.

"She says she was in the bedroom, playing with her new stuffed animals," Maya said. "She got the phone and was pretending they were calling her friend Sophie to invite her to a tea party. Then the door opened and a man was there. She's pretty sure it was one of the men from the woods—one of the men who hurt her mom and dad. She screamed and ran into the bathroom and locked the door."

"Smart girl. Tell her she did the right thing."

"I told her. She says the man tried to get in, and she dialed 911 and hid in the bathtub. The man stopped trying to get in and she waited for me to come get her."

"He may have heard the sirens approaching and decided not to stick around," Gage said. He pulled his phone out of his pocket. "I'll get a team out here to dust for prints. Maybe we'll get lucky." Luck hadn't been on their side much in this case, although the killer hadn't succeeded in getting hold of Casey. He studied the blood clotted in Maya's hair. "Do you want me to get someone out here to look at your head?"

She touched the back of her head and winced. "No, I'll clean up the blood and take a couple of aspirin and I'll be fine." Her eyes met his. "Except now I'm terrified that this guy is going to come back."

"He won't find you here," Gage said. "I want you to come back to my place with me. At least until we can find you a spot in a safe house."

He expected her to argue, but instead, she looked relieved. "That sounds like a good idea."

"What's going on here?" Paige stood in the door of the bedroom, Travis behind her.

"I didn't find anyone in the other rooms," Travis said.

"Someone came into the house, hit Maya over the head and tried to grab Casey," Gage said. He looked at the little girl, who was focused on the pink rabbit. "Casey was smart enough to lock herself in the bathroom and call 911. She says the guy who was after her was one of the men who killed her parents."

"They know Casey can identify them," Maya said. "As long as they're out there, she's not safe."

"We weren't able to get much of a description from her earlier," Gage said. "It's more difficult with children anyway, and with Casey being deaf, well, I guess you could say the language barrier gets in the way."

"Let's get her with a police sketch artist," Travis said. "Maya can translate. With patience, we might be able to coax a good image from her."

"Only if Casey agrees," Maya said. "I don't want to upset her any more."

"Let's find the artist, first," Travis said.

"Are you saying someone broke into my house?" Paige asked. "How?"

"Let's take a look."

"We're coming with you." Maya picked up Casey and followed the others down the stairs.

Gage examined the front door. "This was closed, but unlocked when I got here," he said.

"I know I locked it when I left," Paige said. "I always do."

"It was locked when Casey and I got here," Maya

said. "I opened it with my key, and I know I locked it back." She had a clear memory of turning the dead bolt after she closed the door.

"It doesn't look as if anyone has tampered with the lock," Gage said. He closed the door again and turned to Paige. "Who has the key?"

"Guests are given a key when they check in," Paige said. "And I have one, of course. But that's all."

"Let me see your key," Gage said.

She handed over a silver key ring with what was obviously the key to a vehicle and a silver house key. "It would be pretty easy for someone to take this to a locksmith and have a copy made," he said. "Where do you keep the keys?"

Paige led them to a desk in a small office just off the dining room. She took a key from the top drawer of the filing cabinet and unlocked the center drawer of the desk, and took out a small plastic tray with half a dozen keys inside. "They're all here," she said after a quick scan of the tray's contents.

"But it wouldn't be that tough for someone—a guest or someone else who was in here—to get a hold of one of these and have a copy made," Gage said. "I'll ask the local locksmiths, but depending on when the key was made, they might not remember. Meanwhile, you should probably have the locks changed."

"I certainly will," she said.

"I'm taking Maya and Casey to my place, until we can find them a spot at a safe house," Gage said. "They'll be safer there."

"What am I supposed to do if this creep comes back?" Paige asked.

"We'll run extra patrols by here," Travis said. "Get the locks changed."

"And if anyone asks, tell them Maya took Casey back to Denver," Gage said. "That might throw the killer off the track."

"We'll have Adelaide spread the word," Travis said. "She's more effective than the newspaper for distributing news."

"I'll help you with your things," Paige said and took Maya's arm.

The two women and Casey headed back upstairs. Travis turned to Gage. "I can call the Montrose sheriff and he can probably get you a spot in one of their safe houses this afternoon," he said.

"I think Maya and Casey will be more comfortable here for now," Gage said.

"You mean *you'll* be more comfortable," Travis said.

Gage didn't bother trying to deny it. "I don't trust anyone else to look after them the way I will," he said. "The killer or killers are here in this town—our town. I'm not going to rest easy until we stop them, and until we do, I'm going to have a twenty-four-hour guard on Casey and her aunt."

"I've never known you to take the job quite so personally before," Travis observed.

Gage met his brother's eyes with a hard look of his own. "Don't fight me on this," he said.

"I'm not fighting," Travis said. "And who knows—maybe spending more time around Casey will help you gain her trust. The more comfortable she is, the more she'll be able to tell us about the killers."

That would be good, but Gage was really hoping that spending more time with Maya would help him to gain *her* trust.

WHILE CASEY GATHERED up her stuffed animals, Paige helped Maya collect scattered clothes and toiletries and stash them in her suitcase and backpack. "Are you okay with going to stay with Gage?" Paige asked.

"I feel safer with him than I do anywhere else right now," Maya said. She added a sweater to the clothes in her suitcase. "No offense—I don't blame you at all for that guy getting in here."

"I know you don't." She handed Maya a pair of shoes. "Gage seems very serious about wanting to protect you. No one has ever questioned his dedication to his job, but I'd say there's a little more than that at play here."

Maya tugged on the zipper of the suitcase, glad to have something to focus on besides Paige. "He's probably just angry that the killer was here in town, practically right under his nose, evading all his efforts to find him."

"I don't think that's it—or not all of it."

"I don't care why Gage is taking us in, just that he is. At least with a cop watching over us, I won't be afraid to let Casey so much as go to the bathroom by herself."

"I think you should care," Paige said. "And before you pretend you don't know what I'm talking about,

I'll be blunt—I think our commitment-phobic cop has fallen in love with you."

Maya fumbled the suitcase. "That's crazy. We hardly know each other." People didn't fall in love that fast—especially a man who had sworn relationships weren't for him. Yes, Gage had said he "cared" about her—but that didn't mean love, did it?

She hefted the suitcase off the bed. "Casey needs all my energy and attention right now," she said. "Gage knows that."

"While you're devoting yourself to Casey, it wouldn't be the worst thing in the world to have a man like Gage devoted to you," Paige said.

"You're reading too much into this," Maya said. "I need help and Gage is chivalrous enough to want to help, but he hasn't known me long enough to get attached. A week after I've left town, he won't even remember me."

"Hey." Paige grabbed her arm. "Don't say that. I haven't known you long, either, but you're my friend now. If you need anything, I'm here to help. Me and a lot of other people."

What had she done to deserve people like Paige—and yes, Gage—in her life? And what would she have done without them to help her through the past few days? She put her hand over Paige's. "Thanks. That means a lot."

Casey, her arms full of stuffed animals, joined them. She carefully set the toys on the bed and turned to Maya. "Don't forget the cards," she signed. "I want to look at all of them."

In all the commotion, Maya had forgotten about the box of cards townspeople had sent. "Thanks for the reminder," she signed. "We'll get them right now."

Gage and Travis met them at the bottom of the stairs. "We're going out the back door," Gage said.

She flashed him a worried look. "Why? Do you think the killer might be watching the house?"

"I'm just being cautious." He took the suitcase from her hand while Travis picked up the box of cards and Casey's bag.

"Where are we going?" Casey asked.

"We're going to stay with Gage for a few days," Maya said, signing as well as speaking for the others' benefit.

Casey turned and studied Gage. "You mean, like a sleepover?" she asked.

"Not exactly," Maya answered. "We're just going to stay at his house."

"What did she say?" Gage asked.

"I was just explaining that we're going to your house for a few days," Maya said.

"But what did she say to make you blush?"

She debated making up a lie, but why bother? "She asked if we were going for a sleepover."

Everyone around them laughed, and there was no mistaking the glint in Gage's eyes. "Tell her I'm going to keep you both safe," he said.

Maya hesitated. "I don't want her to think there's anything she needs to be afraid of."

"She's a smart kid. Smart enough to know that if the killer broke in here to try to get her, he's liable to come back. I want her to know she doesn't have to worry about facing him alone."

"You're right. I'll tell her. And thank you."

While Maya relayed Gage's message to Casey, he turned to Paige. "Do me a favor and take a look around outside," he said. "I want to make sure no one's keeping an eye on the back door."

The idea that the killer might even now be watching them made Maya's skin crawl. She was grateful Casey wasn't able to hear Gage's words, and she hoped the little girl hadn't picked up on his concern. Paige went outside and returned several moments later. "There's nobody out there," she said. "I even walked all the way around the house."

Gage had moved his cruiser into the alley behind the B and B. He and Travis stowed Maya and Casey's belongings in the back, then bundled them into the vehicle. "I'll check in with you tomorrow," Paige said. "Try not to worry. And remember—if you need anything, you call."

"I will."

On the drive to Gage's place, Casey was cheerful, playing with her new stuffed toys, signing to them and moving the paws of the bear as if he was signing in answer. Her resilience amazed Maya. But was it really healthy? Maybe she was in denial about what had happened and it would all come back to haunt her later.

Gage slowed and pulled into the driveway of a cedar-sided cottage set against a backdrop of tall pines. "Here we are—home sweet home."

The house reminded Maya of a cabin that might

have been home to a miner or a rugged outdoorsman a century before, with heavy stone pillars framing a cozy front porch and a rusty metal roof sloping steeply from a high peak. Inside, the rooms featured honeyed wood floors and lots of natural light from an abundance of windows. "Your room is back here," Gage said, leading them down a hallway to a bedroom furnished with a queen-sized bed with a black iron frame and a small dresser. "You don't mind sharing, do you?" he asked. "Casey could bed down on the sofa, but I thought she'd be more comfortable with you."

"This is perfect," Maya said. "I'll feel better having her close."

Casey tugged on his sleeve and began signing. He looked down at her, raising his eyebrows in question.

"She wants to know if you're going to catch the man who hit me and tried to hurt her," Maya translated. So the little girl hadn't forgotten what had happened.

Gage squatted down so that he was eye level with her. "I'm going to do my best to catch them," he said, enunciating carefully. He glanced up at Maya. "Tell her that—and tell her she was very brave and very smart this afternoon. She did exactly the right thing, locking herself in the bathroom and calling the police. I'm really proud of her. And I know her parents would be proud, too."

Casey's gaze fixed on Maya as she translated, then she turned to Gage and put her arms around him, buried her face in his chest and began to sob. He looked startled for a moment, then gently returned her embrace. "Go ahead and cry, honey," he said softly, rubbing her back. "Maybe that's what you need, after all you've been through."

His eyes met Maya's over the top of the child's head, and something expanded inside of her, a warmth and lightness that made her catch her breath. Here was a man she could depend on—the kind of man who wouldn't lie or expect too much or do anything but be there for her. Was this what love felt like?

And if it was, what in the world was she going to do about it?

Chapter Fourteen

Casey's sobs subsided after a few minutes and she pulled out of Gage's arms and went into the bathroom. Maya was still looking at Gage with that mix of awe and compassion that made his heart stumble in its rhythm. "Your shirt is wet," she said, nodding to the place on his shoulder where Casey's tears had soaked through the fabric.

"It'll dry." He went to the window and checked the locks. "I don't think anyone saw us driving over here, and we can trust Paige and Travis not to spread the word. We're putting an extra officer on duty to keep an eye on the B and B, in case the man who attacked you comes back."

"This is crazy," she said. "Casey is just a little girl. Why would anyone want to hurt her? But why would anyone want to kill Angela and Greg? None of this makes sense."

He turned away from the window and saw that she had wrapped her arms around herself, as if trying to ward off a chill. "Come here," he said.

"Why?"

So I can try to kiss that frown off your face. What would she do if he said that? But with Casey liable to walk back in the room any second, he reined in his desire. "I want to take a look at your head," he said.

She came to stand by him and he examined the wound on the back of her head. Blood had crusted in the roots of her hair, and she flinched when he touched the swollen lump. "Sorry," he said. "Do you want to take a shower and clean that up?"

"Yes." She glanced at Casey, who came out of the bathroom and began arranging the trio of stuffed animals on the bed.

"Don't worry about Casey," he said. "I'll watch her while you're in the shower."

"Have you had much experience with five-year-olds?"

"Pretty much none, but I think I can manage for twenty minutes or so, while you clean up."

She got Casey's attention and signed to her—Gage assumed she was explaining the situation. Casey sent him a look he couldn't interpret, then nodded, apparently agreeing with the plan. Maya gathered her things and went into the bathroom. Casey watched after her, a worried look on her face.

Gage tapped the little girl's arm and motioned for her to follow him into the other room. Now what? He looked around the room for something to entertain a child. There was television, but that struck him as a cop-out. And would she really enjoy the show if she couldn't hear it?

Inspiration struck. He picked up a pillow and pointed to it, eyebrows raised in a questioning look. Casey looked doubtful, then made a sign with her hands. He tried to imitate it, which elicited a fit of giggles. She made the sign again, more slowly. A gesture like someone cradling a pillow to her head. That made sense. He copied the gesture and she nodded and gave him a thumbs-up.

Gage set aside the pillow and picked up a book. Casey put her palms together, then opened them, as if she was opening a book. All right! That was easy. He copied her and they were off. For the next fifteen minutes, he would pick an object, Casey would demonstrate the sign for that object and Gage would do his best to copy her, his efforts rewarded with a mixture of giggles, frowns and encouraging nods.

Maya, hair still damp and smelling of a floral soap, appeared in the doorway. "What are you two doing?" she asked.

"Casey is teaching me sign language," Gage said.

Casey signed to Maya, her fingers moving too rapidly for Gage to follow. Obviously, he still had a lot to learn.

"I asked her if you're a good student," Maya said.

"What's the verdict?" he asked.

"She says you're pretty good."

"Tell her I have a good teacher." His sheriff's department phone rang. "I have to answer this," he said, and went into his home office.

"Hey," Travis said when Gage answered. "How are things going?"

"They're going good. Casey's teaching me sign language."

"That's good. I called to update you on the report from the Bear's Den. The techs didn't find anything to point to our killer."

"I wasn't holding out much hope that they would."

"No," Travis agreed. "The attacker knew enough to wear gloves, and none of the neighbors noticed him entering the B and B. People go in and out of there all the time, so one more person would be pretty much invisible—especially if he had a key."

"We'll try the local locksmiths," Gage said. "But I'm not holding out much hope."

"Also, I got the report on Henry Hake's car," Travis said. "Thought you'd want to hear it."

"Sure. What did they find?" He leaned back against the desk. Casey's laughter drifted from the other room. Amazing how she could laugh, after all she had been through.

"Hake wasn't in the car and neither were his prints," Travis said. "It had been wiped clean."

"Any idea how long the car had been down there?" Gage asked.

"Nothing certain, but long enough for the leaves on the tree branches it broke on the way down to turn brown."

"So it could have been down there since shortly after he disappeared."

"That would be my guess. I'm going to try again to get in touch with the men who invested in the resort. According to Hake's assistant, they called a lot of the shots from behind the scenes. Maybe he had a dispute with one of them that went wrong."

"They're refusing to talk to you?"

"So far, they've avoided me altogether. The numbers I have go to phones that aren't answered, and there's no way to leave a message. I haven't been pressing it, but now I will."

"I still need to make it out to check on those two guys Wade told us about," Gage said.

"I sent Dwight out to look for them this afternoon, but he hasn't come up with anything yet," Travis said. "Not that Wade gave us much to go on. And we have plenty of other things to keep us busy. We can't afford to be a man short anytime, but especially right now."

If Travis was trying to make Gage feel guilty, it was working. "Tomorrow, Maya and Casey can hang out at the station while I get some work done," he said. "They'll be safe there."

"I've located a police artist who has a lot of experience working with children," Travis said. "His schedule is open tomorrow. If we can get Darla back over to serve as interpreter, maybe they could meet tomorrow. But that only takes care of one day."

"I know. Just give me until tomorrow, at least, to figure something out. Maya was talking earlier about going back to Denver."

"She'll need to go back sometime," Travis said. "She has a job. And Casey is probably in school."

"Yeah." The idea of Maya leaving—and of Casey leaving, too—tore at him. "I'd feel better about them in Denver if I knew they were safe."

"If this guy—or guys, since Casey said there were two of them—are still hanging around town, we're going to catch them," Travis said. "They're going to make a mistake. Though it would help if we knew if this was a random killing, or if it had a connection with something Angela and Greg Hood were involved in."

"We're going to have to dig deeper into their backgrounds," Gage said. "That's something else I can start working on here."

"Good idea."

They ended the call and Gage returned to the living room. Maya was brushing Casey's hair as the little girl played with her stuffed animals. "Everything okay?" she asked.

"The technicians didn't find any evidence at Paige's place." He sank into the recliner opposite them. "The man who attacked you probably wore gloves."

"I wish I had seen him." She shook her head. "He came up behind me so fast."

"Travis is looking for an artist to work with Casey. In the meantime, it would help if we knew if your sister and her husband had a previous connection with the killers."

"I've been wracking my brain, but I can't think of anyone who would have wanted to kill them."

"Who did they purchase that mining claim from?" he asked.

"It belonged to an elderly couple in Boulder—a professor, I think. He had owned the land for a long time, since he was young. It wasn't listed for sale. Greg researched land around here and thought this was exactly the kind of place he wanted, so he visited the man and persuaded him to sell."

"How old was he?"

"In his late eighties—almost ninety, I think."

Then he probably hadn't decided to go after the Hoods. "Did he have children or grandchildren who might have objected to the sale?"

"No. That was one of the reasons Greg was able to persuade him to let it go. He planned to leave most of his estate to charity, and he agreed that cash would be a better gift to leave than these mining claims that couldn't even be built on." She laid aside the brush and patted Casey's shoulder. The girl sat back on the sofa, stuffed toys hugged to her chest, watching the adults.

"I'm starting to feel bad, keeping you away from your job."

"Don't. And what about your job? When do you have to be back?"

"I talked to my principal yesterday and let him know what's going on. Right now I'm on bereavement leave, then I'm entitled to parental leave to get settled in with Casey. That will bring me almost to the end of the semester. We agreed I should probably wait and start again with the new semester in January. It will mean I have to dig into my savings, but I'll be okay. I'm grateful I'm able to take the time."

"What about Casey's schooling?" he asked.

"She's in kindergarten, but I'm not worried about her falling behind." She smiled down at the little girl. "She's already reading simple books and counting. She loves learning and is very smart."

"I can tell."

Casey began signing. "She wants to know if we can have pizza," Maya translated. She put a hand on her stomach. "I just realized we never had lunch. I was making it when all the commotion happened."

Gage stood. "We can definitely have pizza. We even have a good place that delivers." He turned to Casey. "What kind do you like?"

He couldn't interpret her signing and looked to Maya for answers. "Some words don't have a symbol in American Sign Language," Maya explained. "So you do what's called finger spelling—spelling out each letter. She just told you she likes pepperoni."

"I'm impressed," he said. "That's a pretty big word for a five-year-old."

"Well, she misspelled it, but she was close enough I understood," Maya said. "I have this theory that ASL makes kids—and probably their parents, too—better spellers. But I could be wrong. Anyway, if you really want to learn ASL, start memorizing the alphabet. If you don't know the sign for something, you can always finger-spell. It's awkward, but you'll get your point across."

"Good to know. Any other requests for the pizza?"

"Just pepperoni. It's my favorite, too."

"One pepperoni pizza coming up."

BY THE TIME the pizza arrived, Maya was beginning to feel more relaxed than she had since coming to Eagle Mountain. Yes, there was still too much unsettled in her life, and she could never forget that Casey was still in danger. But for whole minutes at a time, she was able to put aside her grief and fear and simply be with Gage and Casey.

Though Casey stayed close, the child seemed less sad and silent than she had been earlier. She continued to sign to Gage and laugh at his awkward responses. Those giggles were like a balm to all the ragged edges in Maya's spirit.

They followed up pizza with more signing lessons, and then Maya noticed Casey's eyelids beginning to droop. No wonder, considering the past couple of days she had had. "I think it's time for a bath and then bed," she signed.

Predictably, Casey tried to argue. When Maya wouldn't budge, she tried a different gambit. "I'm supposed to have a story at bedtime," she signed.

"What did she say?" Gage asked. "Why are you frowning like that?"

"She's asking for a bedtime story," Maya said. "I don't suppose you have any children's books around here."

He actually turned and studied his bookcase, as if someone might have stashed a copy of *The Poky Little Puppy* there when he wasn't looking. "I'm not seeing anything," he said. "But go ahead and give her a bath and I'll see what I can come up with."

She hauled a reluctant Casey to the bathroom, the

little girl's spirits improving when Maya added a generous dollop of bath gel to the water, creating satisfying bubbles, with which Casey amused herself until her fingers and toes were well wrinkled. Maya toweled her off and helped her into pink pajamas.

In the bedroom, they found Gage waiting, a hardbound book in his hand. "What have you got there?" Maya asked.

"It's a photo album my mom gave me a couple of Christmases ago." He sat on the edge of the bed and opened the book. "She made one for each of us kids."

Casey slid under the covers, then leaned forward to study the first pictures. Maya sat on Casey's other side and leaned over her. The picture was of three children—two boys and a girl—each on horseback. "Is that you?" Maya asked, pointing to the middle child, who clearly had Gage's eyes.

"That's me and Travis and our sister, Emily. I thought I'd tell a story about growing up on the ranch, and you can translate."

Casey clapped her hands at this news, and her fingers began flying. "She wants to know what your horse's name was and if you had cows," Maya asked.

"The horse was named Rusty. I got him when he was three and I was ten. He still lives on the ranch. And we had plenty of cows. Hundreds of them."

Maya listened, as enthralled as Casey, as Gage told about growing up on a cattle and horse ranch near Eagle Mountain, doing chores around the ranch, riding horses, exploring old mines and having what sounded like an idyllic childhood. As Gage flipped through the album, pausing over pictures of him and his siblings and parents and a series of orphaned calves, stray dogs and injured birds Gage had nursed back to health, she got a sense of a fun-loving but intensely compassionate kid who had grown into a man determined to right wrongs and defend the defenseless.

By the end of the album, Casey's eyes were closed, and she only murmured sleepily when Maya and Gage each kissed her good-night. Leaving the light in the adjacent bathroom on as a night-light, Maya switched off the lamp and she and Gage tiptoed from the room. He put his arm around her and she leaned into him. *I could get used to this,* she thought. Another voice warned her that this wasn't her real life—not the one she belonged in, where she lived in the city and taught school and did her best to raise her niece without the help and protection of this small-town lawman. Gage was a wonderful man, but she didn't really belong in his world, or he in hers.

"Can I get you anything?" Gage asked. "A glass of wine or some tea?"

"No, I'm fine." They sat next to each other on the sofa. "I can't thank you enough for all you've done for us," she said. "I know part of it's your job, but—"

He put his hand over hers, silencing her. "You know this isn't just about the job," he said. "I wanted to help. I only wish I could do more."

Her eyes met his and the pull of something deep inside of her drew her to him. She tilted her head up and his lips found hers, and a tension she hadn't even acknowledged eased, like a flower bud breaking open.

He pulled her close, his heat enveloping her, his heartbeat a strong, steady rhythm against her chest. Desire burned off the last remnants of inhibition and suddenly all she wanted—all she *needed*—was to be close to him, to love and be loved and to let that love obliterate all the worry and fear and uncertainty that had come to define her life.

He pulled her over into his lap, one hand cradling her hip, the other caressing her breast. She arched to him, the evidence of his desire hard against her thigh. He trailed kisses along her jaw, then pressed his lips to the pulse at the base of her throat. She slid one hand between the buttons of his shirt, fingers brushing across the hair on his chest, a thrill piercing her.

"You know I want you." He spoke the words against her throat, his voice a low growl.

"Yes." It was all the speech she could manage, her senses overwhelmed. He brushed his hand across the tip of her breast and she moaned and shifted against him, aching to be closer still.

His hand stilled, and he rested his forehead on her shoulder. "Maybe we should go into the bedroom," he said. "We don't want Casey coming out and finding us like this."

Casey! Guilt doused all passion like a bucket of icy water. How could she have forgotten about Casey? She pushed away from Gage. "If she wakes up and comes looking for me, I can't risk her not finding me," she said.

The lines around the corners of his eyes deepened and he looked pained, but he nodded. "You're right." He eased her off his lap. "Sorry. Lousy timing."

"It's not your fault," she said, chilled already without his warmth. She had a sudden flash of a future full of moments like this—of passion cooled by the weight of her responsibilities. Not that she had ever had a very active love life up until now, but being responsible for a small child seemed to limit her opportunities even more. Not every man was likely to be as understanding as Gage.

"I don't know whether to be flattered or concerned that you look so sad," he said.

She shook her head, trying to banish the sorrow that threatened to overwhelm her. "I was just thinking about all the things that are going to change in my life now," she said. "I mean, I've known things would be different since I got your call about Angie and Greg. But I think the reality of that is only just now beginning to sink in. And I'm also realizing how much I don't know—how much I can't anticipate."

"My dad always told me, 'Don't borrow trouble,'" Gage said. "Don't worry about things that haven't happened yet." He caressed her shoulder, and she fought the urge to lean into him again. "You're a smart woman. When the time comes, you'll make the right decisions."

"I'll make the decisions," she said. "And hope they're right." But what was the right decision with Gage? If she only had herself to think about, she might risk a relationship with this cop who had a reputation for never being serious—the small-town guy who didn't fit with her big-city life.

But this wasn't all about her anymore. She had to make the right choices for Casey, too. And the little girl needed stability more than anything right now. She didn't need new situations and new people in her life. Maya stood. "I think I'd better say good-night."

"Good night." Gage didn't reach for her hand or try to pull her back. Instead, he let her walk away, into the bedroom, where she closed the door behind her. Did it cost him anything to let her go so easily? Earlier, she had sensed he was struggling, but maybe she had only been projecting what she wanted. After all, in a few days when she went back to Denver, he would return to the life he had always known, while her life would never be the same again.

Chapter Fifteen

The next morning, Maya and Casey accompanied Gage to the sheriff's department, where someone had converted one of the conference rooms into a kind of playroom, with art supplies, games and toys. Adelaide met them at the door with a little girl about Casey's age. "This is my granddaughter, Rhea," Adelaide said. "She wanted to come play with Casey today." Adelaide leaned closer to Maya and lowered her voice. "I explained to her that Casey can't hear, but you know children—they'll find a way to get along."

"Thank you for bringing her," Maya said. She made introductions and the girls headed for the piles of art supplies. Maya settled into a chair at the conference table while Adelaide sat across from her.

"How did it go at Gage's place last night?" Adelaide asked.

"It went fine."

"He seems to think a lot of you and Casey." The older woman studied her, like a bird watching a juicy bug. What did she expect Maya to say—that she and Gage had enjoyed a night of torrid lovemaking? Was she hoping for gossip about Gage's prowess in bed?

"He's been a big help to us," Maya said. "It was kind of him to open his home to us." Certainly, she had felt physically safer with Gage than she would have at the B and B—though the man unsettled her emotionally like no one she could remember.

"He and his brother are two of the finest men you'll ever meet," Adelaide said. "I can't tell you the young women in this town who have set their caps for Gage, but the best of them haven't managed to hold his attention for more than a few months."

"Gage doesn't think a long relationship is a good idea with his job." Maya repeated the words Gage had told her. Had he been trying to warn her off, even then? What had happened to change his mind—or had she been misreading those signals, too?

"A man in Gage's position needs a wife and family to ground him," Adelaide said. "To give him a reason to come home at night and to remind him that being careful is a good thing. It doesn't mean he can't do a good job. Family is the best reason in the world to do their job."

Obviously, the older woman had a lot of opinions about what Gage—and probably Maya, too—needed. Time to steer the conversation in another direction. "How long have you worked for the sheriff's department?" she asked.

"Seven years. My husband was an officer here for almost thirty years. He retired and a year later, he died of a heart attack. I was about half-crazy, sitting around our house all alone with nothing to do, so when I heard the woman who had this job was quitting and moving out of state, I came down and told the sheriff at the time that he ought to hire me."

"Wasn't it hard, being married to a man who might be killed every time he went to work?" Maya couldn't believe she had asked the question—she hadn't even been aware of the thought until she blurted it out.

Adelaide shifted, crossing her legs. "It was if I let myself think about it too much," she said. "But look at how he did end up dying—that could have happened if he was a baker or an accountant or anything."

"I guess you're right," Maya said. "I hope Gage finds the right woman." That was the appropriate thing to say, wasn't it? The timing was all wrong for the two of them, so she should wish he would find happiness with someone else—though the thought made her stomach tighten and her fists clench.

"What about you?"

Maya stared. Was Adelaide suggesting *she* was the right woman for Gage?

"You've got that girl to raise now. Do you have a man back in Denver you could see yourself settling down with?"

"Oh. No, I'm not seeing anyone."

"I'm not saying you couldn't do a fine job raising her on your own," Adelaide said. "Plenty of women—and men, too, I imagine—do a fine job by themselves. But if you can find someone to love and share the burden, it's a help and a comfort."

"Casey needs all my attention right now. I don't have time."

"So you're going to wait until she's grown before

you look twice at a man? Haven't you heard of multi-tasking? I'll bet you do it all the time already. You're a teacher, right?"

"Yes." What did that have to do with anything?

"If you can handle a class full of kids, some of whom don't even want to be there, I think you've got plenty of energy to deal with a little girl and a man."

The phone sounded and Adelaide stood. "I'd better answer that. If you or the girls need anything, let me know."

The two little girls, giggling, worked together on a poster-sized drawing of what might have been a zoo full of animals. A curly-haired woman with a bucket in one hand and what might have been a carrot stood in front of the giraffe, a big smile stretched across her face. A monkey swung from a tree behind her and a big-eared elephant arched his trunk over her head. That was the woman Maya wanted to be—serene and happy in the face of chaos.

She wanted to be a size four with perfect hair, too. Life didn't always give people what they wanted. Right now, she wanted Gage to find the killer who had murdered Angie and Greg, who was threatening Casey. She wanted Casey to be safe and maybe, one day sooner rather than later, to be happy. Then she could start to think about her own happiness.

HENRY HAKE'S HOME was the sort of stone and cedar chalet favored by wealthy second-home owners—a combination ski lodge and mini-mansion, with soaring beams, antler chandeliers and expanses of double-paned glass that looked out on the aspen-studded slopes of Mount Rayford. Travis drove his SUV past the open black iron gate and parked on a paved driveway, the concrete scored to look like cobblestones.

"The place looks deserted," Gage said when he stood beside his brother in front of the oak double doors at the front of the house. Dried leaves had collected in front of the door and old pollen dusted the windowsills.

"My guess is, Hake hasn't been back since he disappeared," Travis said. He pulled on a pair of latex gloves and took a key from his pocket. "State patrol sent a couple of officers out here after Hake's office manager reported him missing, but they didn't find anything suspicious."

Gage, also gloved, followed his brother into the house. A stone-floored entry opened into a great room with a double-sided fireplace and oversized log furniture with thick leather cushions, red-and-green wool throws draped artfully here and there. What looked to be a genuine grizzly bear rug stretched in front of one side of the fireplace, and bookshelves soared almost to the ceiling between the massive windows. Gage gave a low whistle. "Hake lived here by himself?"

"His assistant said he entertained a lot—clients and investors." He moved across the room to a door on the other side and opened it.

"What are we looking for?" Gage asked.

"Any information about those investors or the silent partners he had in the Eagle Mountain Resort project,"

Travis said. "Hake's assistant swears she doesn't know their names and she never met them."

"Do you believe her?"

"She hasn't given me any reason not to. She seemed genuinely distressed by Hake's disappearance and has been cooperative." He crossed the room to a dust-covered desk.

"I take it you've already searched his office," Gage said.

"I would have, but the assistant told me Hake moved all the business files here to his home office, about a week before he disappeared. The plan was to shut down the other office space and run everything out of here. He paid her a generous severance package. She was packing up the last of the office furniture and supplies when she called to report him missing."

"What is she doing now?" Gage asked.

"She moved to Colorado Springs and has a new job." Travis tried the top drawer of the filing cabinet that sat behind the desk, but it wouldn't budge.

"Is there a key in the desk?" Gage asked.

Travis opened the middle drawer of the desk and rifled through the contents. Gage turned to study the open shelving along the opposite wall. Not much of interest there—some copy paper, a paper cutter, box of envelopes, half a dozen books. He walked over and pulled one of the books from the shelf. "*The Deadliest Game—Chemical Warfare in World War II.* Looks like Hake was interested in military history," he said, seeing that the other titles on the shelf also dealt with different aspects of the war.

"I found the key." Travis held up a pair of small gold keys held together with a loop of wire. He turned and fit one of the keys into the top drawer of the filing cabinet. The drawer slid open easily.

Too easily. The two brothers stared at the empty drawer. Travis opened the other three drawers—all just as vacant. "Why bother locking an empty filing cabinet?" Gage asked.

"According to the Colorado State Patrol investigator's report, made the day after Hake's disappearance was reported, this cabinet was full of files pertaining to Hake's businesses," Travis said. "At the time, they didn't think anything in here was relevant to what they were considering a case of a man who had left town of his own accord for a while, but the report definitely mentions them."

"And now they're gone," Gage said. "Who took them?"

Travis's eyes met his. "Maybe the person who put Hake's car in that ravine."

AT ELEVEN THIRTY, Darla joined Casey and Maya in the conference room-turned-playroom. "The sheriff told me what happened after you left here yesterday," she said. "How are you doing?"

"I think I'm more shaken up by the whole thing than Casey is." Both women turned to watch Casey, who, after greeting Darla, had gone back to coloring with Rhea. "She had the presence of mind to lock herself in the bathroom and call 911. Gage thinks the attacker heard the sirens approaching and fled."

"The police artist Sheriff Walker found to work with Casey will be here shortly," Darla said. "I'll translate her descriptions to him and we're hoping together we can come up with a picture to help us identify the culprit. Once he's captured, you'll both feel better."

The door opened and Gage walked in. Maya's breath caught, and her heart fluttered. She had always thought of herself as a woman who would never lose her head over a man, yet being with Gage left her so undone.

"I'm Tim Baker, the forensic artist." A young man she hadn't noticed before, long dark hair tied back in a ponytail, offered his hand. "I'll be working with Casey this afternoon."

"Tim has a lot of experience working with children," Gage said.

"I find that most children, even very young ones like Casey, are very intelligent and know a lot more than we give them credit for," Tim said. "The challenge is finding a way to help them communicate the details they know."

"I imagine it's a bigger challenge when the child is deaf," Maya said.

"Yes, but she does have a language," Tim said. "With Darla as my interpreter, I'm sure I'll be able to understand what I need to create an image of her attacker."

"I'm sure I can help, too," Maya said.

Gage touched her arm. "I thought while Darla and Casey are working with Tim, I'd take you to lunch," he said.

"Children are sometimes more forthcoming when Mom isn't hovering." Tim opened his computer bag and began setting up a laptop. "Since Darla and Casey have already established a relationship, everything should be fine."

Maya started to protest that she wasn't Casey's mother, but Gage interrupted. "Come on," he said. "You could use a break, couldn't you?"

Casey had already turned to greet Darla, who in turn introduced Tim. She barely glanced over when Darla signed that she should say goodbye to Maya, then waved half-heartedly, her attention quickly captured once more by the affable young man. Tim picked up one of the markers the girls had been working with and wrote his name, then drew a cartoon of a penguin that had both girls laughing.

"Rhea, I think your grandmother is ready to take you home," Gage said.

Rhea's eyes said she wanted to protest, but Gage soothed her feelings by putting his hand on her shoulder. "Casey has work to do now," he said. "We'd better leave her to it."

Gage and Maya left Rhea with Adelaide, then walked out to his SUV. "It feels strange to leave her like that," Maya said, looking back toward the sheriff's office.

"She seemed happy when we left," Gage said. "And you can't say she's a timid child."

"No, she isn't," Maya agreed. "She's much more confident than I was at her age—or at any age. How many adults would have the presence of mind to hide from a killer and call 911? Or survive two days and nights alone in the woods? I don't know if I'm cut out to raise a child like that." There—she'd said it—she'd given voice to the fear that had lurked in the back of her mind since news of her sister's death had sunk in. How was she qualified to be a parent? If she had contemplated having children at all, it had been as something that would happen years from now, once she was further along in her career and happily married to the man she wanted to be with for the rest of her life. Even when she had signed the papers agreeing to be Casey's guardian, she had never believed it would happen.

Gage reached over and took her hand. "I'm guessing at some point every parent in the world has thought the same thing," he said. "All parents have to learn as they go. You'll do fine."

"I guess all I can do is try." But his vote of confidence made her feel better. He had a gift for knowing just what to say and do—at least for her.

"What do you feel like eating for lunch?" he asked. "The selection in Eagle Mountain isn't the most varied in the world, but we could run over to Junction if you like."

"I don't want to go to a restaurant," she said.

He went still, though his expression didn't change. "Oh?"

"No. I want to go back to your house." She wet her lips. "To finish what we started last night."

He glanced at her, as if making sure she was serious. Then he keyed the mic on his radio. "This is unit two," he said. "I'm going ten-seven until further notice."

GAGE TOOK HIS cue from Maya and played it cool. He drove to his house, unlocked the door and followed her inside. She deposited her purse on the table by the sofa, then walked back to his bedroom, as if she had done so dozens of times before. When he caught up with her, she was standing just inside the doorway, surveying the king-sized bed with its navy blue comforter, and the simple oak dresser and nightstand. "It's much neater than I expected," she said.

"My mother insisted we make our beds before breakfast every morning," he said. "It's a habit that stuck." He put his hands on her shoulders and gently turned her to face him. "Are you saying you expected me to be a slob?"

"Aren't most people? Trust me, if you had walked into my bedroom unannounced, you would have found the bed unmade and clothes on the floor."

"If I walked into your bedroom unannounced, I wouldn't be thinking about your housekeeping practices." He pulled her close against him. "I'm not thinking about them now."

"So I can tell." She tilted her head up to his in an invitation he wasn't about to refuse. She kissed him back—unhurriedly, with an intensity that stirred him. Her fingers brushed the back of his neck, her nails pressed against his scalp. Her other hand was at his back, fingers splayed across his ribs—or where his ribs were under the tactical vest.

She broke the kiss and pulled back a little. "All this

hardware is sexy in its own way," she said. "But I'm looking forward to feeling you out of it."

He unbuckled his utility belt and set it, clanking, on the dresser, then began unbuttoning his shirt, starting at the top. She tugged the shirt from his waistband and undid the bottom button, working her way up until they met in the middle. He captured her hand and kissed it, sucking the fingers into his mouth one at a time, enjoying the way her eyes glazed and her breath grew uneven. Then he released her hand and stripped off the shirt.

While he removed the vest and the rest of his clothes, she also undressed until she stood before him in bra and panties, both pale pink and relatively plain and as erotic as anything he had ever seen. She had a trim waist and rounded hips and small but full breasts that swelled over the top of her bra, and he couldn't resist cupping her in his hands, smiling when she gasped as he dragged his thumbs across her hardened nipples. "Is this the kind of lunch break you had in mind?" he asked.

"Definitely." She arched against him and he reached around and unfastened her bra and slipped it off. Closing his eyes, he savored the feel of her against him—soft heat and firm curves that made him doubly grateful to be a man here with her right now.

As he pulled the bra out of the way, she walked backward to the edge of the bed, dragging him down on top of her. She stared into his eyes, and he glimpsed need and hope. "Make me forget everything else," she said. "Just for a while."

He did his best to fulfill her request, pleasuring her with his hands and his mouth, learning the contours of her body and reveling in her exploration of his. Neither of them hurried, determined to wring every last drop of pleasure from the moment. By the time he slicked on a condom and positioned himself over her, they were both panting and trembling with need. She welcomed him inside of her and they moved together with both the awkwardness of new lovers and the confidence of two souls who knew each other well. When her climax shuddered through her, he gave a cry of triumph and followed after her.

Afterward, they lay beside each other, silent and sated. If he had had the energy left for words, he would have said he had loved her with all of his being, and she had loved him with all of hers. The idea amazed him. Always before, sex had been about pleasure or release, about having fun and making sure his partner was satisfied as well as himself. He hadn't needed or wanted love to be part of the equation.

"That was exactly what I needed." She rested her head in the hollow of his shoulder, her body curled against his. "I feel like myself again."

"Glad I could help." He caressed her shoulder, keeping his voice light. He needed time to process these new feelings before he bared his soul.

A buzzing from somewhere near the floor disturbed their languid silence. "Is that your phone?" she asked.

"Yes." He sat up on the side of the bed and groped

for his pants. He was composing a tart reply for whoever had interrupted them when he saw that the call was from Travis. "What do you need?" he asked.

"The artist has finished working with Casey," his brother said. "You need to get over here and see this."

Chapter Sixteen

The drawing tacked to the conference room whiteboard showed a burly man with a prominent nose, high cheekbones, sharp chin and lips curled in a sneer. A black knit cap pulled low over his forehead hid his hair, and dark sunglasses obscured his eyes. Maya wrapped her arms around herself and suppressed a shudder. This was the person who had killed her sister and brother-in-law and attacked her? No wonder Casey was terrified of him.

"I did the best I could," Tim said. "But from a child's perspective, this is what a bad guy looks like—larger than life, you might say." He began packing up his supplies. "Casey didn't want to talk about him at first, but we played some games and I got her to loosen up and confide in me. She's a very intelligent child—very aware."

Darla had taken Casey to another part of the station for a snack so the other adults could consult in private. "I hope talking about this man didn't upset her too much," Maya said.

"In my experience, talking about someone they're

afraid of this way—actively participating in efforts to stop him—is very comforting for children," Tim said. "It reminds them the person is human, with a particular kind of nose and a chin and lips and all the little details every other person shares. It demystifies them somewhat."

Gage studied the image, frowning. "It's like a cartoon villain, isn't it—exaggerated features."

"Like I said—larger than life." Tim nodded to the drawing. "He was always wearing the cap and sunglasses when she saw him, which makes it impossible to know details like his hair and eyes. I used my computer program to tone down the features a little and make some guesses on the hair and eyes, but they're just speculation." He picked up a stack of papers from the table and handed them to Gage. Maya moved to look over his shoulder as he paged through half a dozen drawings of men who were similar to, but not exactly like, the drawing on the whiteboard.

"Do any of those look familiar to you?" she asked Gage.

"Yes and no." He set the stack of drawings aside. "There's something familiar about him, but maybe more as a type than as a specific person. We'll distribute the main drawing and see if anyone comes up with anything. Maybe we'll get lucky."

"Even when I have an adult witness who got a good look at a suspect, the drawing doesn't always produce results," Tim said. "People don't always pay much attention to other people, and context matters a lot."

"If you don't think of your brother or your neighbor

as a bad person, it's hard to see them in a drawing of a criminal," Gage said. "Thanks for trying, anyway."

"Yes, thank you," Maya said. "It sounds like you've helped Casey, and that means a lot."

"I was happy to help," Tim said. "Good luck to you."

He left and Gage unpinned the drawing from the board. "We'll get some copies of these made to send out," he said.

"I want to see Casey," Maya said. "I need to make sure she really is all right."

"The two of you will need to hang out here for another few hours," Gage said. "Then we can head back to my place."

Another night at Gage's place, where they would be safe but still so unsettled. As much as she loved being with him, her life wasn't here in this small town. Her life—her job, her home, her friends and everything Casey had ever known—was back in Denver. They needed to get back there, to establish a routine that would help them both to heal.

But as long as a killer pursued them, she didn't see a way for that to happen. They were stuck in limbo and the longer they stayed, the more appealing Eagle Mountain seemed.

Running footsteps heralded Casey's approach. She burst into the room and ran to throw her arms around Maya in a hug. Then she turned and embraced Gage, as well. He looked both surprised and pleased as he patted her back, then awkwardly signed "Hello."

"She certainly has taken to Deputy Walker." Darla

spoke from the doorway. "She told me she's been teaching him sign language."

"She's always been an outgoing little girl," Maya said.

"I think this is more than her natural friendliness," Darla said. "I think she trusts that Gage is going to help her and keep her safe. That kind of security is especially important to her right now."

"I think she'll feel even more secure when she's back home in Denver," Maya said.

"That's when the loss of her parents will hit the hardest, I think," Darla said. "You'll both have to work through your grief. I hope you have friends you can lean on."

Angie had been her closest friend. Maya had never had to go through any difficulty in life without her. She would have to build a new support system for her and for Casey. Why had Angela and Greg ever thought they had needed to buy those old mining claims? If they had stayed home, they never would have run into their killer. They would be alive and their family intact right now.

Casey tugged on her hand. "Come play this game Tim showed me," she signed.

Maya forced a cheerful expression to her face. "Sure," she signed. "That will be fun."

For the next hour, she and Casey played a variation of hangman, in which the object was to guess the word the other player had come up with before a complete face was drawn. Maya could see that this was a clever way to get the little girl to think about the different shapes people's noses, eyes and lips took.

"Did it upset you to talk to Tim about the man who tried to take you?" Maya asked.

"At first I was scared, remembering," Casey signed. "But after a bit it was easier, somehow. And Tim said I could help them stop him from hurting anyone again, and that made me feel good."

"You're the best, bravest girl I know," Maya signed and hugged her close.

"I miss Mommy and Daddy." Casey buried her face in Maya's side.

"I miss them, too," Maya whispered and rubbed Casey's back, trying to comfort both herself and her niece.

Casey fell asleep and Maya sat with her, her mind replaying the events of the past few days, marveling at how much her life had changed in such a short span of time. Later in the afternoon, after Casey had awakened from her nap and resumed scribbling on the drawing pad, Gage leaned into the conference room. "Are you two ready to head back to my place?" he asked. He did a pretty good job of making the signs for "going home," and Casey nodded enthusiastically, her ponytail bobbing.

"I thought I'd grill burgers for supper, if that's okay," he said when they were in his SUV, headed to his house.

"I'll help," Maya said. When he started to protest, she said, "Casey should eat some vegetables, so I'll put together a salad or something."

So they ended up working side by side in the kitchen, while Casey set the table and arranged and rearranged the silverware. It was all so easy and companionable—and Maya told herself not to get too comfortable. This was all temporary, never meant to last.

After supper, they did dishes, then Casey and Gage practiced more sign language. "You've been practicing," Maya said when he successfully ran through the finger-spelled alphabet.

"It's interesting," he said. "And I found a bunch of videos online last night after you went to bed that show a lot of signs."

"He's a fast learner," Casey signed.

Yes, and he had very quickly made a place for himself in their lives. She stood. "Time for you to get ready for bed," she told Casey.

"Can't I stay up a little longer? I want to look at more of Gage's pictures."

Maya translated this for Gage and he held up both hands, a clear sign that he was having no part in this argument. "Come on," Maya signed. "You can have another bubble bath."

This bribe worked, and Casey had her bath and was already yawning by the time Maya helped her into her pajamas. Maya kissed her good-night, then returned to the living room.

"You look like you could use this," Gage said, handing her a glass of wine.

She started to say something flirtatious, about how he was trying to get her tipsy to take advantage of her, or about how he was what she really could use. But she couldn't afford to give in to that temptation. Like pulling a bandage off a wound, she needed to do this quickly, before she lost her nerve. "I've decided tomorrow we need to go back to Denver," she said.

He set his own glass on the table beside the sofa. "I don't like that idea," he said.

"Casey has given you all the information she can, and we need to get back sooner rather than later," she said. "The longer we delay, the harder it's going to be to face starting over without Angela and Greg. And I have so many arrangements to make—for their memorial services, for Casey to move in with me and the legal paperwork for her guardianship." Merely listing it all made her feel overwhelmed.

"I could help you with all of that if you stayed," he said.

"I think I need to handle it myself."

He was silent for so long she wondered if he was angry. Did he think because they had made love she owed him something? Or that because he was a law enforcement officer she should give his judgment more weight than her own?

"If you need anything—anything at all—I'll be there for you," he said.

Some of her resolve melted at the tenderness of his words, but she forced herself to stay strong. "Knowing that you mean that helps more than you could know," she said.

He leaned in to kiss her, but she put up a hand to hold him back. "This afternoon was wonderful," she said. "But I think we had better leave it at that."

He drew back. "All right."

She stood. "It's been a long day and tomorrow will be even longer. Good night."

"Good night."

She lay awake for a long time, listening to Casey's even breathing beside her. She believed she was making the right decision, but why did she feel so awful? Was it because doing the right thing—the adult thing—was all about hard choices and sacrifices? Now that she was a parent, was she facing a life of doing what she should instead of what she wanted?

She wasn't sure when she drifted to sleep, but she woke with a start when Gage shook her shoulder. "Shhh," he whispered before she could cry out. He motioned her to follow him and moved to the door.

Careful not to wake Casey, she sat up on the side of the bed, then stood, still groggy, and trailed him into the living room.

"I'm sorry to wake you," he said. "But I have to go out. There's been another break-in at the school, and one at the outdoor store."

"The same people?" she asked.

"Maybe. A reserve officer will be here any minute and he'll stay with you while I'm gone."

"Do you think that's necessary?" she asked.

"I don't want to take any chances."

A light knock on the door signaled the arrival of the officer. Gage let him in and introduced him, though Maya, still half-asleep, forgot the name as soon as Gage said it. "Don't worry about anything, ma'am," the young man said. "I'll be right out front."

"Thank you," she said.

"I'd better go." Gage leaned in, as if to kiss her, but instead only patted her shoulder. "Don't wait up," he said. "Everything will be fine."

But sleep was the last thing on her mind now. She stood at the window and watched Gage get into his SUV, then located the reserve officer, seated in his patrol car parked at the curb in front of the house. Reassured, she went into the kitchen to make tea. She remembered seeing a chamomile blend in the cabinet when she had helped Gage make supper, and she brewed a cup now. As she stirred honey into the tea, she mused that for a supposedly safe small town, Eagle Mountain was certainly experiencing a rash of crime lately. And people thought cities were dangerous.

The minty, hot beverage soothed her and she began to feel sleepy again. The sight of the patrol car still parked at the curb reassured her, and she headed back to the bedroom and made her way in the darkness to her side of the bed.

But she sensed something was wrong before she had even pulled the covers to her chin. She rolled over and felt the space beside her—a Casey-shaped indentation that was still warm from the child's body.

She sat up and glanced toward the bathroom, thinking Casey had awakened while Maya was in the other room. But the bathroom door was open and the light off. More unsettling, a breeze billowed the curtain of the window on the wall to her right—a window she was certain had been closed before.

Chapter Seventeen

"I can't believe this happened." Wade Tomlinson raked one hand over his shaved scalp. He had met Gage and Deputy Dwight Prentice at Eagle Mountain Outdoors, dressed in camouflage cargo pants, a University of Northern Colorado sweatshirt and sheepskin slippers. "We've been here, what, almost three years, and we've never had any problems."

"Did you have anyone suspicious in the shop in the last day or two?" Gage asked. "Someone who might have been overly interested in one of the items that was stolen, or someone who questioned you about your habits, where you lived, et cetera?"

"No. Nobody like that." Wade shook his head. "I didn't see anybody who might have been casing the place or anything like that."

"What about Brock?" Dwight asked. "Did he mention anyone acting strange?"

"No."

"Where is Brock?" Gage asked. "Does he know about the break-in?"

"I called and left a message on his cell," Wade said. "But he isn't answering."

"Does that surprise you?" Dwight asked.

"Not really. He's been sort of seeing this woman over in Junction. I figure he's at her place, with his phone switched off."

"What is her name?" Dwight asked.

"I don't know. I'm not sure he ever told me." Wade raked his hand over his scalp again and stared at the shattered front window. A large chunk of granite rested in the middle of a display of climbing shoes and technical pants and jackets, pebbles of safety glass like corn snow glinting in the folds of the clothing and along the laces of the shoes. "What am I going to do about my window? Anybody could walk in and take what they want right now."

"Call Tommy Milaski over at the hardware store and he'll open up and sell you some plywood to nail over the window until you can get an insurance appraiser and the glass company out to make repairs," Gage said. He looked up at the camera in the back corner of the store. "That camera should have footage from the area around the cash register, right? We'll need to see that."

Wade's expression grew more pained. "That camera isn't actually connected to anything," he said. "Brock installed it when we opened the store, but he never got around to hooking it up to the computer. He needed to order some component and then we got busy and..." He shrugged. "We've never had problems before."

Gage had heard similar stories from other businesses in town. Either they didn't want to spend the money on a security system or they didn't see the pressing need for one. It made his job more difficult, but as the business owners pointed out, the need for such evidence rarely came up. He consulted the notebook in his hand. "You're pretty sure the only things missing are a pair of climbing shoes and the money that was in the cash register?"

"I'm sure," Wade said. "They couldn't get into the safe, and I didn't see anything out of place. The shoes were right there." He pointed to a gap in the display. "Intense Gravity Escalon, $67.99."

"What size?" Dwight asked.

Wade scratched his head. "Size?"

"If the thief took them to wear himself, it might help us pin down what size man we're dealing with."

Wade nodded. "They were eights. Kind of small for a man, which is why we used them for a display."

Dwight made a note of this. "We got a couple of shoe impressions from the high school," he said. "Maybe this will match."

"The high school?" Wade asked. "Do you think the same person who took the climbing ropes from the high school hit my store? Maybe it's those two guys I told you about. Did you talk to them?"

"We haven't been able to find them," Gage said. "Have you seen them since the day you and Brock met up with them while climbing?"

"No," Wade said. "And I've been keeping my eyes open for them. Talk about suspicious characters—so you think they hit the high school the other day?"

"Someone broke into the high school again tonight," Dwight said, before Gage could signal him to keep quiet.

"No kidding?" Wade said. "What did they take this time?"

"We're not sure yet," Gage said before Dwight could answer. Al Dawson had showed up for work and found broken windows and called the sheriff's office. Inside, someone had emptied the contents of three fire extinguishers around the gym. They had made a mess, but so far it didn't appear that anything was missing. As Dwight had said, the perpetrators had left a couple of shoe impressions on the edge of the gym floor, but Gage wasn't hopeful they would prove very useful.

"I'll ask Brock if he remembers anything else about those guys," Wade said. "He's better with details than I am. I just—"

Gage's phone rang. Checking the display, his heart sped up when he saw Maya's name. He put a hand up to silence Wade and answered. "Hello? Are you all right?"

"Casey's gone. Someone's taken her." He hardly recognized Maya's voice, ragged with terror.

"Are you all right?" He gripped the phone tighter. "Is the reserve officer there?"

"Yes. He's parked out front. Someone came in the bedroom window while I was in the kitchen." Her voice broke. "Gage, I'm so scared."

"I'll be right there." He ended the call and shoved the phone back in its holster. "We have to go," he told Dwight. "Someone's kidnapped Casey Hood."

MAYA PULLED A jacket and jeans over her pajamas and went to the front door to summon the reserve officer. Maybe she should have contacted him first, but all her instincts had told her to call Gage. He was the one who had helped her before, the one who cared about Casey almost as much as she did. The officer met her at the door. "Gage called and told me what happened," he said, his eyes dark against a pale face. "I don't know how. I was out front, watching the house and the street, the whole time."

"He came in the back," she said. "Through the bedroom window." She started past him, but he took her arm, holding her back. "I just want to see where he came in," she protested, trying to pull free.

"You might destroy evidence," the officer said. "We need to wait for Gage."

They didn't have to wait long. Gage's SUV screeched to a halt behind the patrol car, followed by another sheriff's department vehicle. Gage jogged up the walk and took the steps two at a time to reach them. "Gage, I swear I was watching the house the whole time and I never saw a thing," the reserve officer said.

"Not now, Carl." Gage took Maya by the shoulders and looked her in the eyes. "Are you sure you're okay? Did the kidnapper try to hurt you?"

"I never even saw him," she said. "I was in the kitchen making tea, and when I came back to the bedroom, Casey was gone and the window was open. I know it was locked when I went to bed. I always check and—"

"It's all right." He squeezed her shoulders—more of a caress. "You didn't do anything wrong." The steadiness of his voice and the tenderness in his eyes calmed her.

"I started to go around back to check, but your officer stopped me. He said I might destroy evidence."

"He was right." Gage gave the young officer a nod. "Carl, you stay here with Maya while Dwight and I check out the scene. The crime scene techs are already on the way."

Maya hugged her arms across her stomach and watched as Gage and Dwight made their way around the side of the house. Carl, looking miserable, stood beside her, shoulders slumped, staring at the porch floor. The lights in the houses across the street came on— the neighbors were probably watching out the window, curious as to why three cop cars were parked in front of the house.

Gage opened the front door and stepped out onto the porch. "I left Dwight guarding the scene until CSI gets here," he said. "It looks like the kidnapper cut out a pane of glass, reached in and unlocked the window, then came in and out that way. It probably only took a few minutes."

Some of the shock was wearing off and Maya focused on picturing the scene Gage had described. "Did they plan to knock me out again and take her?" she asked. "Or was he watching the house, waiting for me to leave the room?"

"I think he was probably watching the house," Gage said. "I think the break-ins at the high school and Eagle Mountain Outdoors may have been designed to draw me away from the house so the kidnappers could make their move."

"So we could be talking about an organized group," Carl said. "Not just the person who took Casey."

"That's the way it looked to me," Gage said. "Carl, I need you to take over for Dwight guarding the scene. I need him to follow up on some other things for me."

When they were alone, Gage opened his arms. "Come here," he said.

She went to him, sighing when he wrapped his arms around her and drew her close. She closed her eyes and tried to draw on his strength. As tempting as it was to collapse and weep into his arms, she needed to stay strong for Casey. "I can't believe this is happening," she said. "I feel so helpless. What can I do?"

"Don't give up hope." He pulled back enough to look her in the eye. "I'm sorry they took Casey, but I'm glad you weren't in the room when the kidnapper came through the window. He might have done more than just knock you out."

The impact of his words shook her. "You think he might have killed me to get to Casey?"

"If this is the same person who murdered your sister and her husband, he's already proven he's capable of murder."

"But they didn't kill Casey. Why not?"

"I don't know. But every indication so far is that they wanted to take her alive."

Maya covered her face with her hands. "I can't bear to think what they might do to her."

"Don't." Gage gently tugged her hands away. "Come

with me into the bedroom and tell me everything that happened after I left the house tonight."

She walked with him to the bedroom. The window was still open, curtains rising and falling in the breeze like ghostly dancers. The covers on Casey's side of the bed were pushed back, the faint indentation made by the small body still visible. Gage went to stand beside the bed. "I don't see any sign of a struggle," he said. "She may not have awakened when they snatched her. Or they might have sedated her."

"Drugs?" Maya shuddered.

"It would keep her quiet and make her easier to transport," Gage said. "She isn't a very big child, so a man, or even a strong woman, could carry her back out through the window and across the yard fairly easily. If they had a car waiting on the street behind this one, they could get away unnoticed. We'll canvas the houses on both streets. Maybe a night-shift worker or someone with insomnia saw something unusual."

He moved to the window. "Was it exactly like this when you first saw it?" he asked. "You didn't open it wider or push back the curtains or anything?"

"No. As soon as I realized Casey was gone, I called you."

"We'll get the crime scene techs in here to take pictures and look for trace evidence." He turned away from the window. "Is anything else in the room out of place? Anything missing?"

She looked around, trying to remember how the room had looked when she went to bed. She had folded her clothes and put them on the chair by the door, and

Casey's clothes were on top of the dresser. "Casey's jacket. It was hanging on the bedpost and now it's gone." Hope rose in her chest. "If the kidnapper took the time to get her jacket, that must mean he doesn't intend to harm her, right?"

"I don't know what it means," Gage said. He took out his notebook. "So she was wearing pink-and-white pajamas with some kind of design on them." He frowned. "Princesses or something?"

"Disney princesses. And her jacket is pink, with white trim. It zips up the front and has pockets."

He scribbled in the notebook. "We'll make sure this is part of the Amber Alert." He slipped the notebook back into his pocket and put his arm around her. "I could use some coffee. Could you make me some?"

She recognized the attempt to keep her busy and out of the way, but didn't argue. "Sure. Anything else?"

"Just some coffee would be great." She started to turn away, but he grabbed her hand. When she turned toward him again, his gaze met hers. "We're going to get whoever did this," he said. "We're going to find Casey."

She nodded. "I believe you." Gage would do whatever it took to find Casey. Maya only hoped he found her alive and well, before it was too late.

Chapter Eighteen

The more Gage reviewed the events of that night, the more convinced he became that the break-ins at the high school and Eagle Mountain Outdoors had been designed to get him away from his house, leaving Maya and Casey vulnerable. That pointed to a perpetrator who knew him, and who knew enough about the Eagle Mountain Sheriff's Department to know they didn't have the staff to handle multiple break-ins without calling in Gage. That meant the person would also know that the only officers left to guard Maya and Casey would be less-experienced reserve deputies—officers who were less likely to take the initiative to patrol the property on foot. Gage cursed his own carelessness in not recognizing an attacker might approach from the rear, and that locked windows were no barrier to a really determined criminal.

"Both of the break-ins that night were a lot of flash and noise, but no real substance," he reported the next morning, when every available officer gathered at the sheriff's department for a briefing. "Nothing was taken from the high school, and less than fifty dollars and a pair of climbing shoes from Eagle Mountain Outdoors. There was nothing sneaky about either crime. The thief didn't care if he set off alarms—in fact, he wanted to."

"None of the neighbors around Gage's house saw or heard anything suspicious that night," Dwight reported. "That's not surprising, considering it was three in the morning."

"Not an insomniac or newborn who needed feeding in the bunch," Travis said. "What did CSI come up with?"

"No prints." Gage read from the report he had pulled up on his tablet. "The perp wore gloves—another indication that this was a well-planned hit and not a random grab. Right now, we're operating on the theory that whoever kidnapped Casey Hood is connected with the two men who murdered Angela and Greg Hood."

"That had earmarks of a professional hit, also," Travis said.

"Have we had any results from the drawing Tim Baker did using Casey's description of her attacker?" Gage asked.

"Nothing useful," Travis said. "We've had a few calls from people saying they thought the person shown in the drawing looked familiar—like someone they had seen around town—but nothing concrete that even leads to anyone we could question."

"If these guys thought they needed to silence the kid because she could identify them, why not just kill her, too?" Dwight asked. "Why take the risks involved in kidnapping her?"

"We don't know," Gage said. "But if they believe they

have a reason to keep her alive, that buys us more time to find her." He didn't say what he knew every person in the room was thinking—they were working against the clock to find Casey alive. Time could make the kidnappers change their minds, if they hadn't already.

"So we think the break-ins at the high school and Eagle Mountain Outdoors are related to the kidnapping," Dwight said. "Carried out by accomplices of the kidnappers in order to draw you away from the scene."

"That's the way it looks to me," Gage said. Beside him, Travis nodded.

"What about the earlier break-ins at the high school?" Dwight said. "When the climbing rope and mats, and the lab equipment were taken."

"Hard to say," Travis said. "My instinct is no—those break-ins were to steal specific things. The one last night was fast and loud, with general vandalism and nothing stolen. I think someone knew about the other crimes and figured doing something similar was a good way to get every available officer on scene and away from the vicinity of Gage's house."

"What about the skinheads Wade Tomlinson reported as suspicious characters?" Gage asked. "Do we have anything else on them?"

"We searched the camping area Wade said they were in and talked to other climbers in the area," Travis said. "No one remembers seeing anyone like them around."

"Those types would stand out around here," Dwight said.

"Exactly," Travis said. "I'm beginning to think Wade made them up."

Gage stared at his brother. "You mean he deliberately lied to us? Why?"

"I don't know. Maybe to grab some attention for himself or his business—you know it happens."

Gage nodded, letting the idea sink in. Plenty of people got an adrenaline charge from being involved, even peripherally, in a police investigation. But Wade Tomlinson had always struck him as much more grounded than that. Still, how well did he know the man? They weren't close friends who spent time together. "It's something to consider. Do you think he made up the story about the break-in at his store, too?"

Travis frowned. "Throwing a rock through your own front window is pretty drastic, but we'll be giving him a closer look. I put a call in to the police chief in Butte, where Wade and Brock supposedly worked for an outfitter before they came here to open up shop. We'll see what he has to say."

"What about Henry Hake's disappearance?" Dwight asked.

"What about it?" Gage asked.

"Do you think it's related?"

Gage and Travis exchanged glances. "Why do you think it would be?"

"Timing and proximity, mainly," Dwight said. "The resort Hake wanted to develop was adjacent to the land the Hoods had purchased."

"That might be just coincidence," Gage said. "Hake disappeared weeks ago, and we haven't found anything to connect him with the Hoods or their property."

"Right now, we're treating Hake's disappearance

as a separate crime," Travis said. "And we can't forget
about it while we're dealing with Casey's kidnapping
and the Hoods' murders. We're still trying to figure out
what happened to the files that were in Hake's home
office and if they're related to his disappearance."

"Still, it wouldn't hurt to look for more connections
between Hake and the Hoods," Gage said. The hairs
on the back of his neck had stood up when Dwight
had suggested a connection between Greg and Angela
Hood and Henry Hake. "I'd like to get Maya back in to
take another look at her sister's belongings. Maybe now
that she's had more time to think, she'll see something
significant that she didn't notice before."

"Do it," Travis said. "Meanwhile, the rest of us are
going to be combing every possible camping site and
climbing area, just in case those skinheads Wade described show up."

CASEY OPENED HER eyes to darkness. Her stomach hurt
and she felt dizzy, but gradually she realized she was
in the back seat of a car, which was driving over a
rough road. As her eyes adjusted to the darkness, she
realized the two people in the front seat weren't her
parents, but two men—she had only glimpsed one of
them for a few seconds, but had recognized him as the
man who had tried to grab her at the inn where she and
Aunt Maya had spent the night. One of the men who
had killed her parents. Her heart pounded so hard she
thought it might burst out of her chest, and she had
to bite her bottom lip to keep from crying out from
fear. But she must not let them know she was awake.

As long as they thought she was still out, maybe they would leave her alone.

She tried to think what to do. She had been sleeping so good in the bed she shared with Aunt Maya in Deputy Gage's house when the man had grabbed her. He had put his hand over her mouth so she couldn't scream, then pressed a handkerchief that smelled sweet over her face and everything went black again.

She couldn't see the other man—the driver—very good, but he was shorter and wider than the first man. He was probably the man who had helped to kill her parents. Were they taking her somewhere to kill her? The thought made her feel cold all over, and she started to shake. She tried very hard to keep still. *Think*, she told herself. She had to get away. Aunt Maya and Deputy Gage would find out she was missing and they would come looking for her. She had to stay alive long enough for them to find her.

She closed her eyes again, afraid one of the men in the front seat would look back and notice her staring at them and realize she was awake. Her hands were tied in front of her with some kind of rope. There were several big knots, but the rope wasn't too tight. She could move her hands a little apart. She had small hands and strong fingers, from using them so much to make words, instead of using her voice. She wiggled her hands and moved her wrists. The rope rubbed against her skin and hurt some, but the pain didn't matter, did it? Not if she could get free.

The car made a sharp turn and she had to brace herself to keep from falling off the back seat. It bumped over a very rough road, then came to a stop. Casey risked opening her eyes just a little bit. She watched the two men in the front seat through her lashes. They looked like they were arguing, their faces screwed up in anger, arms waving and fingers pointing.

The tall man in the passenger seat suddenly unsnapped his seat belt, got out of the car and came around to open the back door. He reached in and pulled her out. She forced herself to keep her eyes closed—to let her body go limp and pretend that she was asleep. But the man pinched her—hard—and her eyes flew open. His mouth moved—he had his face close to hers and was saying something, but she couldn't read his lips or understand what he wanted from her.

He picked her up and carried her, long strides moving swiftly across the ground, the second man running alongside them. She tried to see where they were, but had only a glimpse of shadowy trees and a few buildings. Then they were inside one of the buildings—a chilly space that smelled of damp dirt and rusty metal. The man who had been carrying Casey set her on the ground, then shoved her so that she fell over. She hit the ground hard and rolled, her bottom throbbing where she had landed on it. When she looked up, the man had switched on a flashlight and was shining the light all around the room. But she only caught glimpses of a ribbed metal roof and rock walls. Then the man shone the light in her eyes, making her raise her bound hands to try to shield herself from the painful glare.

The light went out, though the ghost of it still blinded her. Casey lay frozen for a long moment, waiting for her vision to clear. When it did, she could make out two shoebox-sized squares of pale light on the dirt floor. As her eyes adjusted more, she saw that the two light squares came from a pair of vents in the ceiling, which was curved and made out of a heavily ribbed metal. Concrete block walls—not stone, as she had first thought—rose up to meet the roof. The floor was dirt, damp in places, a thin trickle of water running down a channel in the center of the space.

The door was a thick slab of metal set at one end of the room. It fit tightly in its frame, not even a splinter of light showing around it. Casey ran to the door and threw herself against it, but it didn't budge. She stood a moment, scanning every corner of the building, which was about the size of the living room at home. She didn't see any place for the two men to hide, so they must have left her here and gone away.

She leaned against the door and worked on freeing her hands from the rope the men had used to bind them. She strained and grunted, ignoring the pain when the rough cord scraped the skin from her thumb. She flexed and bent and tugged until first the thumb, then the rest of the fingers on her right hand, were free. After that, she was able to free her other hand from the binding. She tucked the rope in the pocket of her coat, then went to the far corner of the room and peed in a rusty metal can she found there. Feeling better, she began searching for a way out of the room.

The only openings besides the door were the two air vents, high up in the curved roof, in the center of the room. Casey tried jumping, but she couldn't come close to reaching those openings. The room didn't contain any furniture or any boxes she could stack to climb onto, and there was no ladder. Frustrated, she sat on the floor and stared at the door. She hoped Aunt Maya and Deputy Gage would find her soon—before those two men came back.

"I NEED YOU to look at your sister's things again and see if there's anything, however small, that you don't recognize or that seems out of character or unusual." Gage studied Maya's exhausted face, wondering if he was wasting time with this avenue of investigation. Was he grasping at straws that didn't exist while a killer did away with an innocent little girl?

"I'll try." Maya rubbed her temples. "I've been going over and over the conversations I had with Angie and Greg about this new venture of theirs, trying to remember any details that might help. But everything was very general—they had bought the property, had plans for it as the start of a new business venture and might move to Eagle Mountain because it was a quiet, beautiful place that would be good for Casey."

"Take a look at their belongings again," Gage said. "Now that a few days have passed, maybe something will stand out for you."

She nodded, and he led her down the hall to the

conference room. He watched her while she walked slowly past the tables and the items laid out like the remnants of someone's yard sale, yellow evidence labels standing out against the blues and greens of the camping equipment and clothing. She stopped in front of one of the plastic storage containers and the miscellaneous canned and packaged food arrayed beside it, each item carefully inventoried, including a trio of glass jars with lids. "Angie liked to keep everything in these glass canning jars," she said, picking up one that was filled with shriveling red berries. She squinted at the jar. "What are these?"

Gage leaned over her shoulder to get a closer look at the contents of the jar. "I think the tech said they're rose hips. Wait a minute." He consulted the evidence sheet on a clipboard by the door. "Here it is—approximately one pint of fresh rose hips. Well, not so fresh anymore."

Maya set the jar down. "I'm sure she read somewhere that rose hips are good for something. She was always experimenting with new recipes and jellies and things." She glanced at Gage. "What are rose hips, anyway?"

He pulled out his phone and did a search on the term. "'Rose hips are the fruit of wild roses, valued as a source of vitamins A and C and other vitamins and minerals.'" He looked up from the phone. "She must have found some wild roses on their place and picked these." Except he had tramped over pretty much every square inch of the Hoods' land searching for Casey and didn't remember any roses. He did, however, have a clear memory of the rose hedges alongside Henry Hake's property—hedges heavy with blooming roses, thorns…and fat, red rose hips.

Chapter Nineteen

Maya felt the change in Gage, a sudden tightening along his jaw and straightening of his shoulders, almost like a dog that has alerted on a scent. "What is it?" She gripped his arm. "You've thought of something, haven't you?"

"I'm not sure. Just an idea where your sister might have gotten these. And a connection to another case. I'm wondering if while picking these rose hips, your sister and her husband saw something they shouldn't have."

"Tell me," Maya said. "Could the kidnappers have taken Casey there? Where is it?"

"I can't tell you, but I promise we're going to check it out. Right now. You can stay here and wait, or I'll take you to Paige's place and you can wait with her."

"I'm done with waiting," she said, not suppressing the anger that rose at his suggestion. "If you find Casey, she's going to need me—not a bunch of officers who will mean well but who won't know how to communicate with her. When you find her—and I'm refusing to accept that you won't—you'll need to know what she knows right away. It could make the difference between catching these men and not."

He frowned, but she knew he couldn't deny the strength of her argument. "You'd have to follow orders and stay out of the way."

"I could do that. You know me enough now to know that I won't go all hysterical or try to interfere. But I need to be there for Casey."

"Let me talk to Travis," he said.

"Talk to me about what?" The sheriff, shadows under his eyes and in need of a shave, joined them in the evidence room.

Gage glanced at Maya, clearly debating whether to say anything in front of her. "There's no sense keeping anything a secret from me," she said. "Don't waste any more time."

Gage turned to his brother. "Angela Hood was picking rose hips some time not long before she was killed." He picked up the canning jar and showed it to Travis. "I'm thinking she was around that big rose hedge on Henry Hake's property. Maybe she and her husband saw something they shouldn't have."

Travis arched one eyebrow. "Such as?"

"I don't know. But if Henry Hake's kidnappers took him there to hide him—or to kill him—maybe the Hoods were witnesses and that's why they were killed."

"And maybe the killers took Casey there," Maya said. "There are all kinds of buildings on that property, aren't there? What if they took her to one of them?"

"Can we get a warrant for a search based on a jar of rose hips?" Gage asked.

"With Hake and Casey missing, and the Hoods' murders right next door?" Travis nodded. "Judge Wilson would probably be sympathetic." He clapped Gage on the shoulder. "Grab Dwight and anyone else on duty and head up there. I'll get the request for the warrant to Judge Wilson and let you know as soon as it's a go."

Travis headed for his office. Gage locked up the room, then radioed Dwight. "Get as many officers as you can round up and meet me at Eagle Mountain Resort. As soon as we get the go-ahead from Travis, we're going in."

She followed him down a long hallway to a room with a heavy steel door. He unlocked it and she found herself in a small space filled with weapons, ammunition and even a battering ram. Gage scanned the array of items, then pulled a black vest from a box. "Put this on," he ordered.

Putting on the vest brought home the seriousness of the situation. It was hard and heavy and the fact that he felt she needed to wear it frightened her more than the rifle and ammunition he took from the room. But she pushed down the fear and followed him back out of the room to his SUV.

"You stay in the vehicle," he said as he started the engine. "If I tell you to get down, you get down."

"I will."

The grim expression on his face tore at her. "Gage, you know I don't blame you for anything that's happened."

His jaw tightened. "I should have realized an attacker could approach from the rear of the house," he said. "I should have stationed another officer there."

"You can't anticipate everything—" she began.

"It's my job to anticipate. To protect the people I care about."

The words rocked her back in her seat. Of course, she knew Gage cared. His every action had said as much. But to hear the sentiment spoken out loud touched her deep inside. She reached over and took his hand. "That means everything to me," she said.

He didn't look at her, but he squeezed her hand and held on to it as they drove out of town. Whatever happened next, they would face it together.

THE SUN WAS sending a pink stain over the ash-gray sky as the officers assembled before the gates of Eagle Mountain Resort. The feathery branches of lodgepole pines and white fir looked black in the smoky light, and the air smelled of evergreen. Gage parked his SUV with the bumper up against the gates. Travis had worked quickly, and Judge Wilson had okayed the warrant before Gage was out of cell phone range.

"Unbuckle your seat belt in case you need to get down quickly," he told Maya.

She did as he asked and looked at him, her face very pale, the blue ends of her hair bright in the dim light. Ridiculous hair, but he loved it. He loved pretty much everything about her, yet he had to lock all of that emotion away for now. If he didn't, he would be too afraid for her to do his job.

"Be careful," she said. "Maybe I'm not supposed to say that, but I will, anyway."

"You can say it. And I'll be careful." He thought

about kissing her, but settled for giving her a long look he hoped told her everything he couldn't say, then he got out of the SUV and went to meet the rest of the team.

"We've got a warrant to search this place," he said. "Every building." He indicated the pair of bolt cutters Dwight had pulled from his cruiser. "If it's padlocked, cut off the lock. We're looking for a little girl, Casey Hood, who was taken from her bed this evening while she was sleeping. If you come across any sign of her, or anything else suspicious, notify me."

They spread out and for the next hour, they combed over the property, peering into storage sheds full of gardening and construction tools, an empty concrete bunker whose purpose Gage couldn't determine and what had once served as the sales office for the proposed resort, the office furniture and filing cabinets it contained coated with a thick layer of dust. The backhoe and tractor parked in a shed at the back of the property was not dust covered, and judging from the tracks leading to it, had been recently used. Elsewhere on the property tire tracks, shoe impressions, freshly cut trees and newly poured concrete attested to recent activity. But they found nothing suspicious, and no sign that either Henry Hake or Casey had ever been there.

The officers reassembled at the gates to the development, most of them looking as discouraged as Gage felt. "This didn't pan out, so go back and start working our other leads," he said. "Circulate that artist's sketch. Canvas the neighborhoods around my house and around the B and B again. Look for anything we've missed."

As they left, Gage returned to his SUV. He inserted the key in the ignition, but instead of starting the engine, he stared at the tall iron gates and the abandoned buildings and crumbling streets beyond. Something wasn't right here. He couldn't shake that feeling.

"We've missed something," he said. "I can feel it." He opened the driver's-side door again. "I want to take another look around."

"Let me come with you," Maya said. "Please."

He hesitated. But in addition to not finding Casey, his men hadn't found any signs of danger. "Okay," he said. "Maybe you'll see something we've missed."

He led the way around the gates and up what would have been the main street. An eerie silence had settled over the scene, not even the birds calling to each other. Their boots crunched on gravel as they turned down a side street, past the air vents, which had turned out to belong to an air tunnel that led into an abandoned mine, the entrance into the main adit blocked by a heavy iron gate, the hinges so rusted it was obvious it hadn't been opened in the last decade.

"We searched every building on the place," Gage said, sweeping his arm to indicate the half-dozen structures along the deserted remains of streets. "But I can't shake the feeling we're missing something. Call it cop instinct or a hunch or whatever you like."

"I believe you," Maya said. "I feel it, too. The place looks so harmless, but something isn't right." She turned slowly in a circle, then pointed to the end of the street, where a narrow path led into the underbrush. "What's back there?"

"I walked back there until the path gave out," Gage said. "There's nothing." But he fell into step behind her as she held back the low limb of a tree and pushed into the underbrush.

A breeze stirred the still air, bringing with it the scent of blooming roses. A glance to his right showed Gage the pale pink blossoms on the rose hedge along the edge of the property. The vines climbed eight feet up the fence in a thick tangle of blooms and thorns, impenetrable. In between the blossoms glowed bright red rose hips, like beads scattered from a broken necklace.

Maya had seen the roses, too, and left the path to get a closer look. "Careful," Gage said. "Don't let them stick you."

"Angie must have really wanted those hips to risk picking them out of all these thorns." Maya started to retreat and stumbled, and Gage lunged forward to catch her before she fell. He steadied her, and she stared at the ground at her feet. "I tripped over something metal," she said. "Some kind of grate."

He released her and knelt to feel what was definitely a pair of metal grates. They showed no signs of rust. He unclipped the Maglite from his belt and played the beam across the grating. "Maybe these are for drainage," he said. He tugged at the metal, but it refused to budge. "I've got some tools in the truck—let me get them. I want to see where this leads."

"I'll wait here." Maya looked around them. "Otherwise, we might have a hard time finding this again. It's pretty well hidden back in here."

He hurried back toward his SUV, excitement spur-

ring him into a trot. They'd found something significant, he was sure, though what and whether it would
lead to Casey—or to Henry Hake—he had no idea.
He retrieved a pry bar and a toolbox from his SUV
and hurried back down the path. Despite Maya's fears,
the place where they had turned off the path was easy
enough to find, the brush bent down and crushed by
their footsteps. But he didn't see Maya. Had something
else caught her attention and she had wandered away
to investigate? "Maya?" he called.

Silence was his only answer. Maya had disappeared.

MAYA'S HEAD HURT—a throbbing pain as if someone was using the inside of her skull as a drum. She
moaned and tried to roll over, away from the pain, but
a sharp ache in her right arm made her gasp and open
her eyes. She looked up into Casey's concerned green
eyes. Casey, so sweet and seemingly unharmed. Maya
closed her eyes again, tears leaking out of the corners.
She must be dreaming. Or maybe she was dead and
this was heaven—but then why would her head throb
and her arm ache?

Casey shook her, and Maya opened her eyes again
and sat up. She hugged the girl close and Casey put
her arms around Maya's neck and hugged back. If this
was a dream, she didn't want it to stop.

"Are you okay?" Casey signed.

"I'm okay." She was alive and that was all that
mattered. But on the heels of this thought, panic rose
to choke her. Gage? Where was Gage? She looked

around her at the dimly lit concrete block–walled room. "Where's Gage?" she asked Casey.

Casey shook her head. "He isn't here. The bad men only brought you."

The bad men. Maya massaged her throbbing temples, a memory more painful than the ache in her skull taking shape. Two men grabbing her roughly as she waited for Gage. One of them, the larger of the two, had pulled her arms behind her back and held her while the other one slapped her when she tried to scream. Then everything went black.

"Who are the bad men?" she signed to Casey. "Where are we?"

But the little girl didn't know the answer to either of those questions. "I think they're the same men who killed Mommy and Daddy and tried to hurt us that day at Paige's house. One of them came in the window at Gage's house and brought me here."

The child must have been terrified, left in this concrete bunker alone. Maya pulled her close. "Gage will come for us," she said, then signed the same message to Casey.

After a while some of the panic subsided and she sat back, rubbing her arm where it still ached. "You must have hurt your arm when they threw you in here," Casey signed. "You hit the floor really hard. I hid when they came back, over in the corner." She pointed to a shadowy corner farthest from the door. "But they didn't even look at me—they just threw you down here."

Maya stood and went to the door. There was no knob or latch on this side, and it fit so tightly in its frame that she doubted she could wedge even a knife into the gap—if she was the kind of person who carried a knife around, which she wasn't. "You can't open the door from this side," Casey signed. "The only way out is up there, but it's too high."

Maya looked where her niece pointed and started at the sight of two metal grates. She was sure these were the same grates she and Gage had been standing over. He would have returned to them by now. What would he do when he discovered she wasn't there?

He would do everything in his power to find them. The certainty with which this thought came to her should have surprised her, but when she thought of Gage, she thought of him going without sleep and walking miles through the woods and doing everything he could to find Casey—and then, once she was found, taking the two of them into his own home to protect them.

"Gage will be looking for us," she told Casey. She pulled the girl close again. "We just have to wait for him. As soon as he can, he'll be here."

MAYA HADN'T WANDERED AWAY, Gage knew. She wasn't like that. She wasn't the type to be distracted by a pretty flower, or to strike out on her own. He examined the ground around the grates and the crushed weeds and broken branches testified to a struggle. A strand of blue thread caught on a thorn attracted his attention and he pulled it free. Not thread, but Maya's hair. She had fought with someone here and been overcome.

Gage followed the path of the struggle, moving as

quickly as he dared through the undergrowth. The trail led back to the development, but disappeared when he reached the crumbling asphalt of the street. He scanned the deserted landscape. No sign of Maya. No sign of anyone. He pulled out his cell phone, already knowing he wouldn't find a signal, but needing to be sure. He would have to go back to his SUV and drive down the mountain until he was within range, then call everyone back up here to search. That would take at least twenty minutes—twenty minutes in which whoever had taken Maya could get farther away, or in which they might decide to kill her.

She might already be dead. But he rebelled against that thought. If whoever had taken her wanted her dead, he would have shot her on the spot, the way he had killed Angela and Greg Hood.

He started down the street at a run, but he didn't get very far. A man stepped out of the empty concrete bunker and turned toward him. Gage stopped and stared. "Wade? What are you doing here?"

Wade Tomlinson's eyes were flat, his mouth set in a hard line. "I was really hoping I wouldn't have to do this," he said. Then, before Gage could react, Wade pulled a gun from his jacket and fired.

Chapter Twenty

The impact of the bullet sent Gage staggering back, pain radiating from the center of his chest. Wade fired again, striking lower and Gage fell, grappling for his sidearm. He freed the weapon from its holster and fired, the shot soaring wide. He struggled onto his knees and aimed at Wade's fleeing figure, but before he could squeeze off a shot, someone tackled him from behind. An arm like an iron bar pressed against his windpipe, and a big hand wrenched the pistol from his grip.

"I shot him twice. Why isn't he dead?" Wade came running up, panting.

"He's wearing a vest, you moron." Brock Ryan's clipped voice sounded loud in Gage's ear. Gage fought to free himself, but it was like trying to wrestle with a gorilla. Then he went still as the barrel of a gun—maybe his own weapon—pressed against his temple.

"Don't! Someone's coming!" Wade looked over his shoulder. Gage, fighting to remain conscious as Brock choked off his windpipe, heard nothing, but Wade grew frantic. "They must have heard the gunshots. We have to get out of here."

"Open the door to the bunker," Brock ordered. Still gripping Gage in a choke hold, he dragged him backward toward the bunker. "We'll leave him with the kid."

"The woman is in there, too," Wade said as he fumbled with the lock.

Brock swore. "What is she doing here?"

"I saw her while I was waiting for you—she was over by the air vents. I had to get rid of her, so I stuck her in the bunker with the kid."

"Why didn't you just kill her?"

Wade shook his head. "I told you before, I didn't sign on to kill women and kids. That business next door with the kids' parents was wrong—it wasn't part of this deal at all."

"You didn't have any trouble taking the money, though, did you?" Brock sneered. He took the cuffs from Gage's belt and clamped them around his wrists, then shoved him into the bunker. When the door had closed behind them, he forced Gage against the wall. Gage gasped for breath, the cool of the concrete against his cheek helping to revive him.

"What did you do with Casey?" Gage asked.

"We didn't kill her," Wade said. "I've done a lot of bad things and never blinked, but I draw the line at shooting a kid."

"Shut up," Brock said, though whether he was addressing Gage or his partner was unclear.

"Why did you kill the Hoods?" Gage asked.

"They were like you—poking their noses where they shouldn't," Brock said. "Search him," he ordered Wade.

Wade patted him down and removed the gun Gage wore in an ankle holster, his pocketknife and baton. When he had stepped back, Brock pressed the gun to Gage's head once more. "Walk!"

Gage walked to the back of the hut, where Brock reached high over his head and pressed something on the wall. A panel slid back to reveal another locked door, which Wade opened. They passed through this door into a rock-lined tunnel so narrow Gage and his captors had to hunch over and shuffle along single file. This opened into another concrete-walled room, lit by bright fluorescent bulbs and filled with what seemed to be laboratory equipment. An astringent smell that reminded Gage of high school chemistry class stung his nose.

He turned his head to try to see more, and Brock jabbed him with the gun. "No sightseeing."

They halted in front of a steel door fitted with a heavy lock. "The boss isn't going to like this," Wade said as he fit a key into the lock.

"By the time he finds out, we're going to be long gone." Brock nudged Gage. "And you'll be dead." Wade eased open the door and Brock shoved Gage hard, almost throwing him into the chamber on the other side. Then the heavy portal closed and locked behind him with a heavy *thunk* that chilled Gage through.

"GAGE!" MAYA RAN forward to embrace him. She had never been so glad to see anyone in her life—to know that he was safe and alive, and that the man who had brought her and Casey here hadn't killed him. At the same time, the knowledge that he was trapped with them filled her with dread. If Gage couldn't save them, who would?

She ran her palms up his chest, the solid feel of him reassuring her, but her fingers snagged on a hole in his uniform shirt. She drew back, horrified to realize he had been shot—not once, but twice. "You're hurt!"

"Just bruised. The vest did its job and saved me." He turned his back to her and extended his bound wrists. "The key to these are in my right front pocket."

She retrieved the keys and unlocked the restraints. Casey bounced up and down in front of Gage, fingers moving rapidly as she signed. "Tell her she's talking too fast for me to understand," he said.

"Slow down," Maya signed.

With an exasperated expression worthy of a sixteen-year-old, Casey slowed her movements. "She wants to know if you're all right and what happened," Maya translated. She handed Gage the key and the cuffs. "I want to know the same things."

He flexed his fingers and rubbed his wrists. "Wade Tomlinson and Brock Ryan got the jump on me," he said. "They're the ones who took Casey, and they murdered her parents."

Maya tried to place the names. "Wade is the man who runs the outdoor store, isn't he?" she asked, picturing the muscular man who had come to the police department to report on some suspicious characters he thought might be responsible for the thefts at the high school.

"Yes. And Brock is his partner. The drawing the forensic artist made from Casey's description resembles Brock. He's a big, imposing guy. And strong as an ox."

Maya stared at the bullet holes in his uniform shirt. "They shot you twice but when that didn't kill you, he brought you here? I'm more than grateful, but why would he do something like that?"

"Brock was going to kill me, but they heard someone approaching and wanted to get me out of sight before they were discovered."

"Are you sure you're not hurt?" she asked.

"I feel like I was kicked by a bull and I'll probably have a couple of major bruises, but considering the shape I'd be in if it wasn't for my vest, I'm doing great." He pulled her close. "Better now that I know you and Casey are okay."

She kissed him, his lips firm and warm against her own, and so alive. She wanted to keep kissing him like this for at least the next several hours, but that was time they didn't have. Reluctantly, she eased back from him.

Casey tugged at his sleeve and signed a question, her movements emphatic, her expression grave.

"She wants to know how we're going to get out of here," Maya said. "The door is sealed tight and the only other opening is up there." She indicated the grates overhead. "I think those are the same ones we were looking at when you left to get tools and someone—I never saw who—overpowered me."

Gage studied the grating, then walked to the back wall of the bunker and started feeling all around. "What are you doing?" Maya asked as she and Casey followed him.

"This bunker is behind the one that's visible at the development," Gage said. "When we searched it earlier, we thought it was just an empty storage space, but it had a hidden door. Brock and Wade opened it and led me through a tunnel to another chamber that was set up like a laboratory. At the back of that chamber was the door to this one." He ran his hands up and down the wall, frowning. "But I think this is the last in the line of structures. Those grates were only a few yards from the fence line, and a few feet beyond the fence is a rock shelf—there's no room for another chamber."

"But what are they doing with all these underground chambers?" Maya asked.

"How much did you see on the way in?" he asked her.

"Nothing. I was unconscious."

"I'm pretty sure that middle space was a laboratory."

"Do you think it's a meth lab or something like that?"

Gage shook his head. "Remember, I told you most of the meth these days comes from Mexico. If Wade and Brock are making drugs here, they'd have to have a way of distributing them. We haven't noticed an increase in traffic on this road, and Eagle Mountain Outdoors is right around the corner from the sheriff's department. We would have noticed any suspicious activity there."

Maya looked at Casey. Even though the little girl was deaf, her lipreading was improving, and Maya didn't want her upset by their conversation. But Casey was over by the door, tracing her finger along the faint crack between the door and its frame. Maya turned back to Gage. "Is that why they killed Angie and Greg? Because they found out about the lab?"

"I'm not sure," Gage said. "Brock said they were killed because they had been nosing around where they didn't belong. That makes me believe they saw something they shouldn't."

"We have to get out of here, or we'll die here, too," Maya said. "Maybe we can wait by the door and when they come back, we can overpower them."

"I don't think they're coming back," Gage said. "At least, Brock said they were leaving."

Panic clawed at her throat as she absorbed these words, but she fought against it. "We have to get out of here," she said again, her voice shaking only a little.

Casey hurried to them. She pointed overhead and began signing. Almost immediately, Maya began shaking her head. "No," she signed in reply. "I won't let you."

"What is she saying?" Gage asked.

"She says we should lift her up and she can crawl out of the grate and go for help. It's a ridiculous idea. Much too dangerous."

Gage tilted his head back to study the opening. "She's the only one of us who could fit through that opening," he said. "If we could get one of the grates out of the way. But we couldn't budge them from the outside." He looked around. "There's nothing we could use for a ladder, but if I boosted you onto my shoulders, you could lift her up."

"Gage, no! It's too dangerous." She took a step back from him.

His eyes met hers. "It's dangerous, but it's not impossible. And it may be our best chance."

"She's only five. How is she going to get all the way into town by herself? And what if she runs into Wade or Brock on the way?"

"She's the smartest, toughest five-year-old I ever met," Gage said. "And she doesn't have to get all the way to town. She just has to get to Jim Trotter's place at the end of the road."

Maya hugged her arms over her stomach, aware that Casey was watching this debate—and aware that everything Gage said made sense. "None of this matters if we can't get the grate loose," she said. "And how are we going to do that?"

"If you stand on my shoulders you can see if you can get it loose from this side."

"Oh, well, if it's that easy, why didn't I think of it?"

"Come on," he said. "Take off your shoes and get on my back. From there, you can climb up onto my shoulders. I promise I won't let you fall."

Skeptical and yes, a little afraid, she nevertheless did as he asked, aware that they were out of other options. She owed it to them all to at least try. She kicked off her shoes and removed her socks as well. Then Gage bent over. "Hop onto my back," he said. "Then you can crouch on my shoulders. I'll straighten up, then you straighten up."

He made the moves sound easy, but they were anything but. "What am I supposed to hold on to?" she asked as she straddled his back, debating her next move.

"I don't know. Maybe—try clasping your hands on my forehead...ouch! My forehead, not over my eyes!"

She moved her hands up, aware that Casey was giggling at the two of them. She managed to plant her feet on his shoulders and crouched there, straddling his head and feeling ridiculous. She was also sure he was risking a back injury and a possible hernia trying to lift her. After all, those gymnasts and ice-skaters being lifted into the air by their partners were usually several inches shorter and many pounds lighter than her.

"I'm going to stand up now," he said.

"Okay." Her voice only quavered a little. She tightened her grip on his head and added a headache to the list of pains she was inflicting on him. He straightened, breathing a little hard with the effort. She crouched on his shoulders, trying to work up the courage to stand.

"You have to stand up now," he said.

"I know. But that means letting go of your head."

"I won't let you fall," he said. "You have to trust me."

Hadn't she been trusting him all this time—to find Casey, to find Angie and Greg's killers, to protect her? Surely she could trust him now to hold her up—or at least, to catch her if she fell. Slowly, she straightened her legs, letting go of him at the last minute, extending her arms for balance. He reached up and gripped her shins, steadying her. When she was standing straight, she let out the breath she had been holding and grinned. "Okay, what do I do now?"

"Can you reach the grate?" he asked. "See if you can move it."

The bottom of the grate was about ten inches over her head. She reached up and grabbed it. It moved a little from side to side, but wouldn't budge up or down. "There are some metal clip-type things holding the grate in place," she said.

"If you wedged something in them, could you break them?" he asked.

"I don't know. Maybe. But we don't have anything to use as a wedge."

"Come down now." Did she imagine the strain in his voice?

She clambered down, jumping the last three feet to the ground. Gage straightened and rubbed one shoulder. "There must be something we can use to break those clips," he said. He patted his pockets and pulled out the handcuffs, a set of keys and his wallet.

"What about a key?" she asked.

He considered his car keys. "I think the metal is too brittle. I've tried to use keys to pry things before and they snapped off." He replaced the keys in his pocket. "But I think you're on the right track. We need something metal and sturdy." He began unbuckling his belt.

She stepped back. "Gage, what are you doing?"

He slipped the belt from the loops of his khaki trousers and handed it to her, buckle first. The oval silver-and-gold buckle with its decoration of a cowboy riding a bucking bronc was heavier than she had expected, the edges tapered. "That buckle is silver with gold overlay," he said. "It should be strong enough for what we need if you can wedge it under the clips."

She turned the buckle over and read the engraving inside. *Gage Walker, Colorado State Junior Champion Bronc Rider, 2006.* "What if I break this?" she asked. "This obviously means a lot to you."

"It's just a belt buckle," he said. He held out his hand. "Ready to try again?"

Now that she had done it once, getting to an upright position on his shoulders wasn't so difficult the second time. She managed to wedge one side of the buckle under the metal clip easily enough, but the clip refused to budge. "Pull down hard," Gage said. "Hang all your weight off of it if you have to. I won't let you fall."

She grasped the buckle with both hands and forced it down against the clip and prayed the sound she heard wasn't the buckle shattering. Something hit her cheek and she instinctively closed her eyes. She almost lost her balance and had to open her eyes, and saw that the bottom half of the clip was gone. "It broke!" she shouted.

"Great! Try the next one."

She managed to break three of the four clips, then was able to reach up and slide the grate to one side, out onto the forest floor. She gripped the opening, debating chinning herself up and trying to wiggle out, but she would be lucky to get more than her head through that small space, much less the rest of her. "I'm ready to come down," she said.

Gage lowered her, and Casey ran up to them. "Lift me up so I can go for help," she signed.

Gage knelt in front of Casey and took her by the shoulders. "You don't have to do this," he said.

Maya translated, but before she had finished, Casey was already replying. "I want to do it," she signed. "I can do it. If I don't, we'll die."

Gage nodded. "All right. I'm going to tell you where to go for help. It's a man named Mr. Trotter. He lives at the end of this road. When you climb out, head for the roses along the fence. Follow that fence to the road and the gate. Make sure no one sees you. When you get to the gate, go left. Do you know left?"

Casey looked from Gage to Maya as he spoke and she translated. She nodded, her expression so solemn that she looked older than five. Maya's heart squeezed, and she swallowed a knot of tears.

"Are you ready?" Gage asked.

Casey nodded. He hugged her close. "That's my girl."

This time, Maya sat on Gage's shoulders and he boosted Casey up to her. The little girl scrambled onto Maya's shoulders, fearless, and was up out of the opening before Maya was really ready. She looked back down at them and waved, then was gone. Maya fought the urge to call after her to be careful. Of course, she wouldn't hear, but it seemed Maya should have done something more than simply let her run into danger that way.

She slid off Gage's shoulders and sagged against him. "I hope we made the right decision," she said.

"We gave her a chance." He cradled her head against his chest. "We gave ourselves a chance. We wouldn't have that without her."

We wouldn't have had anything without her, Maya thought. She closed her eyes and gave herself up to the feel of his arms around her, holding her so close. The search for Casey had initially brought them together, and the shared goal of keeping her safe had forced them to become a team. But what had developed between them—this closeness she had never felt with anyone else—that was something so unexpected, so precious. Out of such great tragedy had come this gift that she didn't know what to do with.

He kissed the top of her head. "Let's sit down," he said. "All we can do now is wait."

Yes, they would wait—for rescue, for a resolution to this whole series of awful events and to see if the love she felt for this man could survive outside of the sadness and need, and become something even stronger.

Chapter Twenty-One

Casey pretended she was a little animal—a squirrel or a bunny running through the woods, hiding from the bigger, dangerous animals. She didn't see anyone else around, but she wouldn't take any chances. She scurried to the rose hedge at the fence, the pink petals scattered on the ground like confetti, and followed it to the road. The big black gate that had been closed before was open now, and a black truck sat in the drive, little puffs of smoke coming out of its tailpipe. But no one inside the truck. Still, she stayed as far from it as she could, then turned and started down the road.

She passed the place where she and Mommy and Daddy had camped. It was empty now. Someone—maybe Deputy Gage—had taken down the tent and driven the car away. She didn't know where Mommy and Daddy were now. What happened to you when you died? Would she ever see Mommy and Daddy again?

She brushed the tears out of her eyes and kept moving, following the road but staying in the woods at the edge of it. She wasn't a sad little girl; she was a little wild rabbit, hurrying along with an important mission.

Maybe she even had a little cape, with an *S* on it for Super Rabbit. The idea made her smile.

A flash of color on the road caught her attention and she ducked deeper into the woods. She hid behind a big tree trunk and trembled as a truck drove past. The man driving was the big man who had grabbed her from the bedroom at Gage's house and taken her out the window. He was the man who had shot her parents. Her heart pounded so hard it hurt, but he never looked her way.

He was headed back the way she had come. Was he going back to kill Aunt Maya and Deputy Gage? She had to hurry to save them. She started running, ignoring the branches that slapped at her and the prickly vines that reached out to grab her. She ran until she could hardly breathe and her side hurt. But she couldn't stop. She had to get help.

She tried to remember what Deputy Gage had told her. She had to go to a man for help. What was his name? She couldn't remember, but that didn't matter. She didn't need his name to go to him for help. He lived at the end of the road.

The road went up a hill and curved, and at the end of the curve, a driveway cut off to the right. She ran faster, arms pumping, legs pistoning, heart pounding. When she reached the end of the driveway, she saw a little house and a man wearing baggy brown pants and a flannel shirt standing outside of it. He had a big white beard, like Santa Claus. This must be the man Deputy Gage had told her to ask for help.

Waving her arms, she ran toward him. The man's eyes widened. They were very pale blue eyes, in a face that was deeply wrinkled. He dropped the shovel he had been holding and opened his mouth and waved his arms, too. She thought maybe he was shouting. Then he picked up a rock and threw it at her.

Casey stopped and stared. Why was he so angry? She was close enough now to read his lips. "Go away!" he said.

She crossed her arms and shook her head. No. She wasn't going to go away. She needed him to help her. They stood like this for a long while, staring at each other. The man made shooing motions and turned his back to her. Casey moved closer, making the signs for *Help* and *Please*.

He said a lot of things she couldn't understand. She kept moving toward him, one step at a time, the way you were supposed to approach a shy animal. He looked toward the door to his house. Was he thinking about going inside? She mimed making a phone call—everyone could understand that, couldn't they?

He shook his head. No, he didn't understand, or no, she couldn't use his phone. Or maybe he didn't have a phone. Daddy had said something about phones not working up here.

The man was still talking, too fast for her to understand. She looked around and spotted a stick and picked it up and wrote in the dirt. *HELP.*

He stared at the word for a long moment, then moved closer and shrugged, his hands out. She understood that. What did she want from him? How to make him understand?

She grabbed his hand and tugged. To her relief, he

followed. She led him down the driveway. At the road, he stopped, but she pulled harder. She was crying now. She hadn't meant to, but she couldn't help it. The man shook his head, but when she tugged at him, he followed.

After a few feet, she began to run. They might not have much time. The man jogged along after her, until they were both out of breath. She slowed down to a walk and he slowed, too. Alternately running and walking, they made their way back to the big black gate, which was still open, though the truck was no longer sitting in the drive.

Casey put a finger to her lips, signaling the old man to be quiet. He nodded that he understood. She took his hand again and led him along the roses, intending to take him to the opening where the grate had been. Deputy Gage could talk to him then, and tell him what to do.

But they hadn't gone far when the old man put out a hand to stop her. When she looked at him, he put his finger to his lips and pointed to the side. She looked and saw the man who had taken her and the other man who had been with him when he shot her parents. They were talking to a man in a black suit. Not talking— arguing, their mouths open wide and their arms waving around.

The old man took her hand and led her deeper into the woods, then up a slope, helping her over the bigger rocks as they climbed. He moved carefully and she thought probably quietly. Instead of boots, he wore soft moccasins, with beading on the toes. They climbed and climbed, until they reached the top of the ridge and could look down on the three men still arguing.

The old man was talking again, though his head was turned away from her. She thought maybe he was talking to himself. He stared hard at the arguing men, then nodded, as if he had come to a decision. He indicated that she should stay where she was while he moved away. She didn't really want him to leave her, but Deputy Gage had told her he would help her, so she nodded and sat.

He moved over the rocks, crouched low and glancing down at the arguing men every few seconds. Then Casey couldn't see him anymore. She hugged her knees to her chest and wished she knew what those men were arguing about. She didn't see any sign of Aunt Maya or Deputy Gage, so she thought they must still be in the concrete room underground.

The ground shook and she jumped up, startled. The rocks under her feet weren't moving, but she could feel vibrations through her feet, like when she was standing on the sidewalk and a car playing loud music went by. She couldn't hear the music, but she could feel it. She turned to see the old man running toward her, hopping over the rocks, while more rocks—a whole river of rocks—slid down onto the men below. One big rock hit the man who had killed her parents and he fell. The man in the black suit ran away and the other man tried to run, but he tripped, and then he was buried under rocks.

The old man scooped up Casey and scrambled with her to the road, where he finally put her down and stopped. He bent over, hands on his knees, breathing hard, but grinning. Casey waited until he straightened, then she took his hand and tugged him toward the grates in the woods.

A questioning expression on his face, he followed her. When she knelt beside the grate and looked down, he did the same, and then he was talking to someone down below—Deputy Gage and Aunt Maya. Casey lay back on the ground and looked up through the lacy leaves to the patch of blue sky above. Darla had told her she believed Mommy and Daddy were in heaven, where they could watch over her. Casey hoped that was true. She hoped they had seen how she had been brave and had gone for help—how she had saved them all.

"CASEY MUST HAVE turned right out of the driveway instead of left," Gage said as he and Maya and Casey stood with Travis by the gate to Eagle Mountain Resort, watching a rescue crew work to remove the ton of rock that had come down off the ridge when Ed Roberts set off the rock slide.

"They were arguing about killing you two, and the little girl, too," Ed said. When Travis and the rescue crew showed up, he had tried to leave, but Travis had persuaded him to stay and give an official statement. "I was just trying to stop them, though I ain't sorry they're dead, after what they did to that young couple and tried to do to the little girl."

"We're not pressing charges," Travis said. "We're grateful for your help."

"You saved our lives," Gage said, and offered his hand.

Ed hesitated, then took it. "I need to be getting back to my place now," Ed said. "I've had enough of all these people and commotion."

"You can go," Travis said. "And thanks again."

Ed left, and Travis went to consult with the rescue team, who had uncovered Wade and Brock's bodies.

"It's over," Maya said.

"Almost," Gage said. "We'll need to get a formal statement from Casey, verifying that Brock and Wade were the men who killed her parents and kidnapped her. I wish I knew what they saw that led to them being murdered—maybe it was something to do with that laboratory."

"Will you be able to tell what the laboratory was for?" Maya asked.

"We'll call in the DEA for that. And we'll be looking for the man Casey and Ed saw with Wade and Brock. He had something to do with all this." He turned to face her. "What will you do now?" he asked.

"I need to go back to Denver and settle Angie and Greg's estate, arrange for their memorial service and all the legal paperwork for me to become Casey's guardian."

"And then?" he asked.

"And then, I don't know."

He caressed her shoulders. "Stay. I know you think Eagle Mountain is a small place that will limit your opportunities, but there's a lot here for you."

"I know that now. You're here."

He kissed her, a gentle caress of his lips against hers that managed to say more than words.

When he lifted his head, she stared up into his eyes—the kindest eyes she had ever known, burning now with passion for her. "Do you think I can do it?" she asked. "Find a job and a place to live and…"

He touched a finger to her lips. "You'll find a job. If not teaching, something else. As for where you'll live…how about with me?"

"Oh, Gage, I don't know. Casey…"

"Casey can live with us, too. I'm asking you to marry me."

"Marry you?" Her eyes widened.

"I know it's sudden, and if you insist, we can have a long engagement. But I love you and I know it's real, and I want to be with you for always—and to be a father to Casey."

"What happened to the man who didn't make commitments? Who thought relationships and being a cop don't go together?"

"I had to find a commitment worth making, and the relationship that was the right fit. I've found both with you."

She looked into his eyes and saw her future there, building a life together with this man who filled in the pieces of her life she hadn't even known were missing. "Yes," she said. "Yes, I'll stay in Eagle Mountain and yes, I'll marry you and yes, we'll be a family. Together."

* * * * *

Get 4 FREE REWARDS!

We'll send you 2 FREE Books plus 2 FREE Mystery Gifts.

Harlequin® Intrigue books feature heroes and heroines that confront and survive danger while finding themselves irresistibly drawn to one another.

FREE Value Over $20

INTRIGUE

*When Annabelle Clementine returns to
Whitehorse, Montana, cowboy Dawson Rogers helps his
ex-girlfriend sell her late grandmother's house to ensure
her swift departure, but first they must solve a mystery...*

Read on for a sneak preview of Hard Rustler
by New York Times *bestselling author B.J. Daniels.*

As her sports car topped the rise, Annabelle Clementine looked
out at the rugged country spread before her and felt her heart
drop. She'd never thought she'd see so many miles of wild
winter Montana landscape ever again. At least, she'd hoped not.

How could she have forgotten the remoteness? The vastness?
The isolation? There wasn't a town in sight. Or a ranch house. Or
another living soul.

She glanced down at her gas gauge. It hovered at empty. She'd
tried to get gas at the last station, but her credit card wouldn't
work and she'd gone through almost all of her cash. She'd put in
what fuel she could with the change she was able to scrape up,
but it had barely moved the gauge. If she ran out of gas before she
reached Whitehorse...well, it would just be her luck, wouldn't it?

She let the expensive silver sports car coast down the mountain
toward the deep gorge of the Missouri River, thankful that most
of the snow was high in the mountains and not on the highway.
She didn't know what she would have done if the roads had been
icy since she hadn't seen a snow tire since she'd left Montana.

The motor coughed. She looked down at the gauge. The
engine had to be running on fumes. What was she going to do?
It was still miles to Whitehorse. Tears burned her eyes, but she

refused to cry. Yes, things were bad. Really bad. But—

She was almost to the river bottom when she saw it. At a wide spot where the river wound on its way through Montana east to the Mississippi, a pickup and horse trailer were pulled off to the side of the highway. Her pulse jumped at just the thought of another human being—let alone the possibility of getting some fuel. If she could just get to Whitehorse…

But as she descended the mountain, she didn't see anyone around the pickup or horse trailer. What if the rig had been left beside the road and the driver was nowhere to be found? Maybe there would be a gas can in the back of the pickup or— *Have you stooped so low that now you would steal gas?*

Fortunately, she wasn't forced to answer that. She spotted a cowboy standing on the far side of the truck. Her instant of relief was quickly doused as she looked around and realized how alone the two of them were, out here in the middle of nowhere.

Don't be silly. What are the chances the cowboy is a serial killer, rapist, kidnapper, ax murderer…? The motor sputtered as if taking its last gasp as she slowed. It wasn't as if she had a choice. She hadn't seen another car for over an hour. For miles she'd driven through open country dotted occasionally with cows but no people. And she knew there was nothing but rugged country the rest of the way north to Whitehorse.

If there had been any other way to get where she was headed, she would have taken it. But her options had been limited for some time now.

And today, it seemed, her options had come down to this cowboy and possible serial killer rapist kidnapper ax murderer.

Don't miss Hard Rustler *by B.J. Daniels,*
available September 2018 wherever
Harlequin® Intrigue books and ebooks are sold.

www.Harlequin.com

SPECIAL EXCERPT FROM

*Hawk Cahill let down Deidre "Drey" Hunter
once before. He isn't going to make that mistake again,
especially since she just married the wrong man—a man
who is suddenly missing.*

Read on for a sneak preview of
RANCHER'S DREAM,
*the next book in **THE MONTANA CAHILLS** series
by New York Times bestselling author B.J. Daniels.*

You will die in this house.

The thought seemed to rush out of the darkness as the house came into view. The premonition turned her skin clammy. Drey gripped a handful of her wedding dress, her fingers aching but unable to release the expensive fabric as she stared at her new home. A wedding gift, Ethan had said. A surprise, sprung on her at the reception.

The portent still had a death grip on her. She could see herself lying facedown in a pool of water, her auburn hair fanned out around her head, her body so pale it appeared to have been drained of all blood.

"Are you all right?" her husband asked now as he reached over to take her hand. "Dierdre?" Unlike everyone else she knew, Ethan refused to call her by her nickname, Drey

"I'm still a little woozy from the reception," she said, desperately needing fresh air right now as she put down her window to let in the cool Montana summer night.

"I warned you about drinking too much champagne."

He'd warned her about a lot of things. But it wasn't the champagne, which she hadn't touched during the reception. He knew she didn't drink, but he'd insisted one glass of champagne at her wedding wasn't going to kill her. She'd gotten one of the waiters to bring her sparkling cider.

So it wasn't alcohol that had her stomach roiling. No, it was when Ethan told her where they would be living. She'd assumed they would live in his New York City penthouse since that was where he spent most of his time. She'd actually been looking forward to it because she'd grown up in Gilt Edge, Montana, and had never lived in a large city before. Also it would be miles from Gilt Edge—and Hawk Cahill.

She'd never dreamed that Ethan meant for them to live here in Montana, at the place he'd named Mountain Crest. All during construction, she'd thought that the odd structure was to be used as a business retreat only. Ethan had been so proud of the high-tech house with its barred gate at the end of the paved road, she'd never let on that she knew the locals made fun of it—and its builder.

When Ethan had pulled her aside at the reception and told her that they would be living on the mountain overlooking Gilt Edge in his prized house, Dierdre hadn't been able to hide her shock. She'd never dreamed… But then she'd never dreamed she would be married to Ethan Baxter.

Don't miss RANCHER'S DREAM
by B.J. Daniels, available now wherever
Harlequin® books and ebooks are sold.

www.Harlequin.com

Copyright © 2018 by Barbara Heinlein

HEATHER GRAHAM

**returns with the next story in her thrilling
Krewe of Hunters series**

NEW YORK TIMES BESTSELLING AUTHOR

HEATHER GRAHAM

KREWE OF HUNTERS

PALE as DEATH

"A thrilling, dark and deadly tale."
—Booklist, starred review,
on Haunted Destiny

The crime scene is horrific: the corpse of a young actress, drained of blood and cut in two. LAPD Detective Sophie Manning's new case is high profile and difficult—there's no evidence to work with. And it's a disturbing echo of the infamous Black Dahlia killing. Sophie is burning the candle at both ends, desperate to catch the murderer before he strikes again, when she starts to experience inexplicable visits...from ghosts.

Bruce McFadden has a particular talent that can help Sophie—he can speak with the dead. As a consultant for the FBI's paranormal team, the Krewe of Hunters, he's been tasked with Sophie's case and they're forced to partner up. But Sophie doesn't want his help, and she doesn't want to share his peculiar skill. And she certainly isn't ready for love, despite Bruce's attentions.

As the killer taunts the police, Sophie and Bruce will discover that the threat is closer to home than they'd ever realized. Working side by side is the only way they'll stop this deadly sequel.

Available now, wherever books are sold!

Be sure to connect with us at:
Harlequin.com/Newsletters
Facebook.com/HarlequinBooks
Twitter.com/HarlequinBooks